"They called him the Cajun . . ."

Slago was sitting on the bed, holding a bottle in his huge hand and staring at nothing at all.

"What's the matter?" Mark asked uneasily.

Slago muttered something to himself, then chopped at the air viciously with his hand. "I was remembering another guy who was there that day. Maybe he ought to be on our list. Maybe we ought to pay him one of our visits." Slago's eyes glittered in anticipation of another brutal beating and the final slashing with his big knife. Then he looked disappointed. "But I don't remember his name."

"It was Durell," Mark said. "Sam Durell. They called him the Cajun. But he wasn't around that day. Forget him. He doesn't have anything to do with this."

Other Original Gold Medal Books in the
"Assignment" Series by Edward S. Aarons:

Assignment • • • •

ANGELINA

EDWARD S. AARONS

An Original Gold Medal Book

GOLD MEDAL BOOKS
Fawcett Publications, Inc., Greenwich, Connecticut
Member of American Book Publishers Council, Inc.

Chapter One

M ARK drove the Cadillac right into town. Corbin objected, in his usual, mild manner, but Mark said it didn't make any difference, because the town was just a gas station and a few ghost shanties in the middle of the Arizona desert. Since Mark gave the orders, there was no further discussion.

Slago sat in the back with Corbin. He looked massive, sweating with eagerness now that the operation was actually begun. Jessie sat up front with Mark. She looked cool and sleek, unaffected by the desert sun, her yellow hair bound up with a narrow blue ribbon she had bought in a five-and-ten in Tucson. Corbin had wanted his wife to sit with him, and have Slago up front, but Jessie had blandly ignored him. Mark, feeling Jessie's warm thigh roll against him as he turned a curve, looked sidewise at her and smiled; but she wasn't having any. Now for the first time, he was struck by the cool detachment she was able to maintain.

"There it is," Slago rumbled. He thrust his round head forward. He had cropped his salt-and-pepper hair in Tucson, and you could see the sweat on his scalp through the short bristles. "Tom Everett. Look at the dump, will you? He was always a jerk, that Tom, remember? Readin' cowboy stories all the way across Europe. He always wanted to come to the West and ride the range, he said." Slago laughed thickly. "So he's a gas jockey in the middle of a stinkin' nowhere. Tech corporal, he was. Always in my hair. No goddam good when the tanks came into the Bulge."

"Did he run?" Corbin asked. His German accent showed a clinical interest. His gray eyes looked opaque behind his rimless glasses. "Is this Everett a coward?"

"Don't make no difference." Slago grinned, and his broad, brutal face shone with anticipation. "He won't be nothing, soon."

"It's fourteen years," Mark said. "Maybe he won't know us."

5

"Ah, he'll remember me," Slago said.

None of them was as young as they had been in the old days, Mark thought. He himself was thirty-eight, and he had called himself Mark Fleming for so long now that he had almost forgotten the name he'd once had, the one on the records up in Ossining. But Jessie made him remember some times in Antwerp and Paris, in that long-ago past. He felt her soft thigh roll against him again, but he didn't want to get Erich Corbin sore. They had been aiming for this a long time, and he didn't want to spoil it because of the blonde. Even if Jessie was twenty years younger than Erich, and had that look on her face and in her pale violet eyes that told him she was willing, he had to remain aloof to keep Corbin happy.

After all, it was Erich who had bought the car, and it was Erich's plans that had started the whole thing. He still needed the little chemist, Mark decided. Later on, if things worked out, he could think about changing the setup.

Tom Everett's gas station looked shabby, crushed by the desolate desert heat, small against the purple mountains on the horizon. A new highway had by-passed the town ten miles south, and there was no other traffic on the road. Mark slowed the heavy Cad reluctantly, because he enjoyed driving the luxurious car. There were two pumps, and a screened door stood ajar in the gray shack beyond. A faded Coca-Cola sign hung askew on its steel stand. There were some weatherbeaten frame houses nearby, ranging the road, but they all looked deserted. A wire cattle fence stretched across the cactus and sage flats beyond the highway, but it was bent and neglected. Nobody was in sight. Liquid heat pools shimmered in the distance. Mark tapped the horn ring, and the sound was lost in the vast, hot silence that closed around them.

A door slammed somewhere in the back of the station shack, and Slago sat up, his broad face alert. Tom Everett came around a corner of the shack, eating a sandwich. Mark knew him immediately. The man was seared by the desert he had yearned for, the juice of youth crushed out of him. But there was no mistake about it. They had the right man. The first on the list. Maybe they'd be lucky and have to go no farther.

6

"Hey, Tom," Mark called softly.

"Fill her up, folks?"

"Don't you remember me, Tom? And the sergeant, back here?"

Everett was tall and thin, with straw hair bleached white by the sun. He had a bony, ingenuous face. He had been the butt of platoon jokes because of his omnivorous reading of Western pulps, and his ambition to get out of Jersey City and live in the West had been universally derided. His faded blue eyes looked confused as he stared at Mark.

"Lieutenant? Lieutenant Fleming?" A slow grin spread over the freckled face. "Glory, it's been a long time! Think of meetin' you here!" His voice lifted and he called, "Mary! Mary, here's some friends I told you about!"

Mark said quickly: "Don't call your wife, Tom. Not yet."

Slago said: "We didn't know you were married, cowboy."

"Oh, sure, I'm married." Everett sounded different when he addressed Slago. His grin was not quite as happy. He sounded a bit cautious, remembering. "Been married for ten years now."

"Where is she?" Slago asked.

"Over yonder, in the second house." Everett pointed. "Let me get her, huh? You got time for a beer and bite with us?"

"Not really," Mark said. "Actually, we looked you up to talk to you." His voice was easy as he felt the car lift as Slago got out and walked casually around the gas pumps behind Everett. "Something has come up," Mark went on. "It's about Metzdorf."

"Metzdorf? Golly, that's a long ways back."

"But you remember it, don't you?"

"Sure." Everett looked puzzled. "What about it?"

"You remember the detail our platoon was on? Bugger-lugging all that paper out of the chemical plant?"

"Yeah, reckon I remember. But we can talk about old times later. You fellows must be powerful dry." Everett seemed to notice the Corbins for the first time. "Maybe the lady would like to freshen up a bit. Your wife, Lieutenant?"

"No," Mark said shortly. Jessie smiled. Corbin frowned behind his thick glasses. "About those files, Tommy."

7

"What about 'em?"

Slago spoke from behind him. "Can we go somewhere and talk?"

"Go somewhere? There's nobody here but me and Mary." Everett began to look alarmed. He no longer seemed happy about the reunion. "What is it with you guys, anyway?"

"We're lookin' for something you swiped, cowboy," Slago rumbled.

"I never swiped anything in my life!" Everett exclaimed. "Look here, you fellows got something awful wrong. Maybe I ain't as glad to see you as I thought. I'm beginnin' to remember some things I wasn't too crazy about in those days."

"Then remember about the files, too," Mark urged gently. He saw the sweat on Everett's bony face, and began to enjoy himself. "Remember Metzdorf, Tom."

"Are you crazy? There's nothing to remember."

"You swiped something," Slago said impatiently. "We were loadin' those files on the truck, and one of the boxes busted. You dropped it and it busted, remember? You always were clumsy, cowboy. And all them papers spilled into the mud."

"I don't remember that," Everett said doubtfully.

"Sure you do. Try."

"I never stole a thing," Everett insisted. "Look, all that happened a long time ago. You fellows come driving in from nowhere and don't even have a beer or anything, you just start giving me the third degree, like. Is it a gag?"

"No gag," Slago said softly, and hit him on the back of the neck, without warning.

Slago, at forty, was still a bull of a man, his shoulders meaty and powerful under the flowered sport shirt he wore. The blow slammed Everett to his knees in the dust in front of the gas pumps. He clawed at the Cadillac's dusty tail fin and Slago chopped at his fingers and Everett rolled away, trying to get up. Slago kicked him in the ribs. Everett started to scream in anguish and surprise, and Slago hauled him up with one hand and hit him in the mouth, starting blood from broken teeth, and then flung him, sprawling, toward the screen door of the station shack. Slago had worked with speed, efficiency, and relish.

8

Jessie got out of the car, her long legs flashing under her full skirt. "Does he have it, Mark?"

"We don't know."

"Let Slago do it, Mark. Do you understand?"

Mark nodded. He could smell her perfume as she put her hand on his arm and watched Slago pick up Everett. She wore a peasant-type blouse and he could see the deep, smooth cleft between her breasts, tanned all the way down. There was some excitement in the way she breathed, but not much. He wished he knew what was going on behind her pale violet eyes.

"Get back in the car, Jessie. Look out for his wife, if she shows up."

"You don't have to worry about me."

"It isn't going to be pretty."

"Maybe I've seen worse."

"Where?" he asked.

She looked at him. Her face was cool and lovely. "You're not very subtle, Mark. Don't ask questions like that."

Mark looked at Erich Corbin. Corbin, still in the Cad, seemed disinterested in the proceedings, and Mark felt a sudden, irrational flash of hatred for the German's cool temperament. He turned away from Jessie and followed Slago as Slago shoved the shattered Everett into the shack.

THERE was no alarm. The empty, weatherbeaten houses down the road were drowned in the silent blast of sunshine. Apparently, Tom Everett's wife was either asleep or out of sight and sound in the back of her house. It was cool in the shack, away from the direct impact of the afternoon sun. A thermometer on the outside wall registered 105, but inside there was an illusion of coolness in the dark shadows. There was a Coke machine, a cigarette machine, a battered cash register, a glass-topped counter thick with dust, containing automatic accessories, sunglasses, candy bars and spark plugs. He felt contempt for Everett, who had dreamed of the glamorous West and had ended like this.

"Now we get the truth out of him," Slago said thickly.

Slago was an expert. Everett had no chance to cry out, and Slago needed no help from Mark. He worked on the man avidly, using fist and knee, and finally a long, bone-handled switchknife.

They didn't get the answer they hoped for.

Everett was still conscious when Mark knelt on the wooden floor beside the gasping man.

"Look, Tom, we know it still exists, even after all these years. We advertised in newspapers all over the country for war souvenirs. For letters with Hitler's signature, for instance. We got all kinds of answers, because we offered good prices, and people collect anything, so nobody paid any extra attention to our ads. And we got one answer we were looking for, in St. Louis. It was signed A. Greene, with just a box number for a return address, but it described what we were looking for. But when we wrote and checked back, we got no answer. And we couldn't find A. Greene. He never even picked up our letter offering to pay for the autographed papers we wanted. But it satisfied us. We know it hasn't been lost or destroyed, even after all this time. One of our squad members stole it from that broken file box in Metzdorf. It still exists. And we want it. We don't really give a damn about the letter with Hitler's signature that was clipped to it. If you want to keep that, fine. But we want the other papers in that folder."

"I don't know what you're talking about." There was a bubbling sound in Everett's throat. His eyes looked vague, then sharpened in focus and reflected a last spark of anger. "You guys won't get away with this, comin' in and beatin' up on me like damn coyotes. I ain't got what you want, but you won't go askin' any of the other guys in the squad, either. I'll see to that. I'm callin' the sheriff . . ."

Slago hit him again. And again. Fifteen minutes later, even Slago was convinced. He was panting and sweating, his sport shirt dark with stains, his face shining with lust for what he was doing. Everett lay crumpled behind the counter, his khaki trousers wet with urine and blood, his face battered almost beyond recognition.

"He ain't got it," Slago admitted. "It wasn't him."

"All right," Mark said. "Finish it. He'll call copper if we let him. And we can't let him tell what we asked him about. There are others on the list."

"What about his wife?"

"Let her find him here. She hasn't seen us."

Slago nodded and took his knife and bent over the

unconscious man. Mark saw the quick, slashing movement of Slago's thick arm as he drew the blade across Everett's throat. He turned away, surprised at the squirm of nausea lifting in his stomach, and walked out into the sun and waited.

Slago came out in a moment.

"The jerk," Slago said.

Jessie and Erich Corbin were still waiting in the Cad. The highway shimmered emptily in both directions. Mark took a small notebook from his coat pocket and flipped it open and tore off the first perforated page on which Tom Everett's name was written.

"Who is next?" Jessie asked quietly.

"We go to Indiana. John Miller."

"That crum," Slago said happily.

So rr was begun. Mark drove the blue Cad east and north, toward St. Louis. Now it was started, there was no way to turn back. Mark had never killed before, except in the war, when his record had earned him a field promotion to lieutenant. He knew it didn't matter that Slago had actually done the killing. They were all equally guilty. Jessie, too, with her cool violet eyes and beautiful body and smooth, blank face. But there wasn't any other way they could make it with safety.

Mark had spent ten years on the Coast in the rackets, working for the narcotics syndicate, gambling, and vice. It had seemed simple and obvious, after the war, when you were familiar with violence and danger. It was the easiest way to make a quick strike and then take it easy like a gentleman for the rest of your life. But it hadn't worked out that way. At one time he had worked the woman angle, taking six thousand from the woman on West End Avenue, taking jewelry from that blonde bitch in Westport, Connecticut. He had the front, the good looks and strength, the acquired polish and easy sociability to do it. But he didn't delude himself. He knew himself for what he was. He had been a gutter animal as a kid, and he could never bury that part of him; he wasn't sure he ever wanted to.

Erich and Jessie Corbin had looked him up four months before, when he had gone to New York from the Coast as a messenger for Big Socks Johnson, a lucky coincidence to be in the East when Corbin was looking for him there. They had already found Slago, working as

11

a teamster for a trucking outfit that fronted for Pat Angeli's rackets. Lucky he had hung around Johnson's place on Fifty-Fourth, the bar where Jessie found him and took him to her chemist husband. Corbin had been in the country almost a year, looking for him.

Mark had turned down Erich's proposition at first, not believing a word of it. Then Erich showed him the missing parts and told him what could be done if they were successful in finding the rest of it. So they started hunting. There was a long road ahead, but Corbin had plenty of money to stake them in luxury. And he seemed patient enough. Even about Jessie.

From the tail of his eye, as he drove the big Cad eastward, Mark saw the long, clean exciting length of her and felt the softness of her hip roll against his. Not for the first time, he wondered why she had hooked up with a mouse like Erich. She was graceful and tall, even for a woman, and she dressed with style, moved and walked with a quiet excitement that was contagious. She needed a lot more than Corbin could give her. And she didn't talk too much. He liked that.

He could see her in the rear-vision mirror. There was a small dew of perspiration on her upper lip, exciting him with the thought of her body under her tan linen dress. She wore large yellow beads, a matching bracelet, and yellow earrings. He liked the way the wind blew her taffy-colored hair and the way it modeled the simple but expensive dress to her body. All at once her eyes met his in the mirror. For a moment they were utterly blank, deep violet. Then she smiled serenely.

"Keep your eyes on the road, Mark." She had a pleasant, deep controlled voice. "Don't drive too fast. It would be stupid to get stopped by a local for speeding."

Her hand rested lightly on his knee as he drove. She knew what he wanted, Mark thought. It would be soon, now.

JOHN MILLER was a building contractor in Harlanville, Indiana. It was flat country, fine for developments, and he had done well in the last ten years. He was even thinking of going into politics. A bachelor, he had a penthouse suite in the Hoosier Arms which would not have amounted to much in New York, but which just about made him top dog in Harlanville. He was a

12

past-commander of the VFW post, active in Rotary and the Lions, and popular with the country club crowd, although he often had to stand still for some ribbing about the quality of the clubhouse, which he had contracted to build. This didn't bother him. The men liked his liquor, and some of the women weren't reluctant about a drive in his car and a late drink up in his suite. He was doing all right. He had put on weight in the past fifteen years, and he had avoided mentioning his fortieth birthday last week. He never gave much thought to the old war in Europe, except when he attended VFW meetings, and even then he thought of it as something glamorous and long ago, with the haze of time mellowing the mad terrors he had known then.

He had the habit of driving every evening to inspect the progress in construction at his newest site. He was a careful man, a cautious bookkeeper, and he always checked the work that had been accomplished by his carpenters and masons. The project was two miles beyond the country club, along the Dearing River, where he had picked up some lush meadowland for a song. The houses were small, rectangular boxes with slab roofs, all identical. They were monotonous and ugly. But they looked beautiful to Miller because he saw them only in terms of profit. He parked his car by the construction shack and walked across the bald, dusty area of what would be the main street of the development.

The evening was sultry, with a heavy quality in the air, a static summer weight that oppressed him. It would rain again soon, and rain always meant delays in his schedule.

He was surprised to see the Cadillac parked beyond the last foundation. And even more surprised to see Sergeant Slago come walking toward him, unchanged after all these years.

Hatred followed Miller's surprise, leaping in full flame from the dark hole where he had buried it long ago. For over a year after being mustered out, Miller had nurtured dreams of meeting Slago somewhere and beating the man until he crawled for mercy. Even now, he was aware of a feeling of guilt, as if he had goofed at some stupid duty ordered performed, and he froze in his tracks to watch Slago walk toward him with that hard, familiar rolling gait.

A gorilla, Miller thought. Hardly changed at all. And

13

in the same breath he knew how much he had gone to fat, soft as a woman in the belly, and even more of a physical coward than he had been during the war. He was frightened.

But Slago smiled, and his handshake was hard and friendly. Miller's guilt and hatred evaporated. He saw Lieutenant Mark Fleming get out of the Cadillac, too, and he felt a small pleasure in the meeting, anticipating his exhibition of civilian success. And this was mixed with surprise and wonder at their appearance here.

Slago wasted no time. Slago asked his questions.

"You're kidding," Miller said. "I don't remember anything about Metzdorf. I wasn't even on that detail."

"Yes, you were," Slago said. "I remember it, all right."

"What difference does it make? It's long dead and buried. You fellows didn't look me up just for that, did you? Listen, come back to town with me and have dinner. We can have a time. I could even get you some women." Jessie and Erich Corbin were not with Mark and Slago this time. They had remained at the motel, five miles west of Harlanville. Miller smiled, then found the effort painful as he saw the bleak look in Slago's eyes. He tried to smile again. "Well, come on, let's not just stand here," he added uneasily.

"We're not going anywhere," Slago said. "Not until you answer us."

"I told you I wasn't in on it. What's so important about Metzdorf, anyway? I don't remember a thing about it."

Slago abruptly began the work he relished. It was easy, softening up this fat pulp of a man. He went slower this time, letting Mark ask more questions between rounds, because Corbin had suggested that perhaps they had rushed things a bit back in Arizona. It was lonely at the unfinished development site. The evening was dark with growing shadows. Under the drooping willows nearby, the river ran placidly on between its banks. Slago didn't worry about Miller's screams; there was nobody around to see or care about it.

In ten more minutes, Mark was satisfied. Slago paused, panting in the evening heat. "Another blank. He ain't got it. He'd spill his fat gut by now, if he had it."

"All right," Mark said. "Finish it."

Slago took out his knife.

14

THEY were a hundred miles from Harlanville before Mark chose a motel for the night. While Slago arranged for their rooms with the proprietor, Mark took out his small black notebook and tore off a perforated page and crumpled it in his fist. He got rid of it by burning it in the Cad's ashtray.

Erich Corbin said: "Who is next?"

"Perry Hayward. New York."

"Very well. We will go there." Corbin touched the glasses on his pinched, white nose. He wore a seersucker suit and a small prim bow tie. "It will be all right, Mark. We will use the same methods. A man in pain will gladly babble the truth. Slago is excellent for the purpose. The letter and the other papers exist; the answer to our ad proves that. One of the men in your squad that day still has it. Perhaps he keeps it only as a souvenir, since not many men have the training in chemistry to recognize the contents of the papers accompanying the Hitler letter." Corbin smiled thinly. "Otherwise, we would have heard of the product before this."

"And if we make a mistake with one of these men?"

"It is up to you to make sure there is no mistake." Corbin's voice was quiet. "True, you could play the part of an old war buddy and visit each man, search his home quietly, ask questions without arousing suspicion. You could talk over old times, and what would be more natural than to inspect any souvenirs laying about? But you would be alone then, *nein?* I could not be a guest with you. And if you learned something, you would learn it for yourself."

Mark looked very dangerous for a moment. "You have a lot of faith in me."

"I have none at all, my friend." Corbin smiled easily. "But do not let that insult your vanity. Millions are at stake, too much for trust to exist between us. Not a bank in the country will be safe. But in order to insure this, as I've told you before, there must be no chance of the police making any connection between these men. Who will remember that they served together, so many years ago? Eliminating them is the only way for us to remain safe."

"I still don't see why it took you fourteen years to come over here after them," Mark said.

15

"And I explained that, too," Corbin said patiently. "I was taken to East Germany and put to work there. I had no chance to escape. But I never forgot, and when the opportunity came, I moved. I am a patient man, Mark. I found you, did I not? So we will find what we are looking for, too. This person, this A. Greene answered our advertisement with a description of the Hitler letter—so we know it still exists." Corbin frowned. "You are concerned because A. Greene did not follow through with the deal and vanished. We must hope that some inconsequential personal affair prohibited his reply to our second letter. But we do know that one of your men picked up those papers when the filing cabinet broke. I saw him do it. And I know they were the papers we want. I have friends in Washington, and they checked the records for me. This one sheet, with the letter attached to it, is missing." Corbin turned and looked at Slago coming out of the motel office. "We must operate on the assumption that the man in your squad who took the paper still has it, or knows where it is. Unfortunately, I was watching from an upper window of the plant. I was virtually a prisoner there. All of your men looked alike in their uniform raincoats. It was impossible to identify him. But I was curious about the man's behavior. So I approached the Military Governor captain and told him the file box had been broken when loading on your truck, and I offered to check to see if everything was in order. I was most cooperative. As soon as I came to the formula papers, I knew that the piece your man took was the one I would need some day. Naturally, I said nothing about it."

Mark wanted a drink. He wished Corbin wouldn't keep repeating what he had been told before. "Well, I hope your pie in the sky makes good eating."

"If we succeed in this first step, all the rest will be simple," Corbin said gently. "Think of the money. All we want, simply for the taking of it. Without danger, without any risk at all."

"I'm thinking of it," Mark said.

M ARK and Slago occupied the motel room next to the one shared by the Corbins. It was a hot night, with the rumble of thunder muttering over the plains of Indiana. Truck traffic roared steadily on the highway nearby. Mark took a bottle of Scotch from his suitcase and filled half a tumbler and drank it slowly while he stripped off his clothes and took a shower. Corbin was right. There was no risk, as long as they were careful. Each man had to be killed. Nobody could possibly connect what had happened in Arizona with what happened in Indiana and what would be in New York.

He stood under the shower until the approaching thunderstorm made him think about the lightning and he got out and toweled and shaved quickly. His round, good-looking face, with the thick, curly yellow hair, looked unchanged in the mirror. He remembered how Miller had gone to fat, how Everett had lost his boyish look and was stamped with dust and defeat. But he hadn't changed much. He could still pass for under thirty, he decided, thinking suddenly of Jessie.

Maybe tonight, he thought.

When he came out of the bath, Slago was sitting upright on the edge of the nearest twin bed, holding the bottle in his hand and staring at nothing at all. "What's the matter?"

Slago muttered something to himself, then chopped at the air with his hand. "I was remembering another guy who was there. You know, in Metzdorf. Remember a G-2 captain who supervised the detail, told us which files to pick out for the War Records Commission?"

"The Cajun, they called him," Mark said.

"Yeah. Maybe he ought to be on your list. But I don't remember his name."

"It was Durell," Mark said. "Sam Durell. But he was nowhere around that day. Forget it."

He went outside and waited for Jessie.

Chapter Two

DURELL closed and locked his desk and dropped the keys into a small compartment in the vault. Then he cleared the manila folder off his desk and put that in the vault, too. Sidonie Osbourn got up and used her key in the vault lock to complement Durell's, and they locked the box together. Sidonie patted his arm.

"Don't look so unhappy, Sam. You'll be back soon."

Durell smiled thinly. "I have the feeling I'm being let out to pasture, honey. Is McFee in?"

"Waiting for you."

"My orders?"

She gave him a sealed envelope. "Here. You be careful, Sam."

"I always try to be."

Sidonie was worried about the anger that darkened his eyes. She knew his temperament; she knew of his loneliness even with Deirdre. He was a dedicated man who would laugh at the thought of being called a devoted patriot. She knew what it meant to him, leaving K Section.

"Have you heard from Deirdre?" she asked.

"I had a phone call from London. She goes to Paris tomorrow. Covering fashions, of all things." Durell tried to keep his voice empty of his irritation. "She won't be back for another month."

"Well, you come have dinner with the twins, hear?"

"I don't know where I'll be," Durell said. "I'll make it if I can, of course. And thanks."

He left his office and walked down the quiet corridor to the elevator. No. 20 Annapolis Street was a graystone building in a residential section of Washington, with nothing about it to indicate it was headquarters for K Section of the Central Intelligence Agency of the State Department. Downstairs were the front offices of a commercial concern that actually procured small-part supplies—nuts, bolts, machine-screws and small optical instruments—for the armed forces. The elevator was the only approach through the steel doors to the upper floors. The place had become home to Durell in the last three years, and he knew this attitude was a mistake. An espionage agent has no home, he reminded himself, and no life he can call his own. That was the basic problem between Deirdre and himself. Scowling, he lit a cigarette in the elevator on his way up to Dickinson McFee's office.

Durell was a tall man in his thirties, with thick black hair, a small, trim mustache and dark blue eyes that reflected the quickness of his Cajun temper. He was powerfully built under his conservative gray summer suit, and he moved with deceptive ease and grace. His fingers were long and slender, adept with a gun, knife, or a hand in a poker game. He had been brought up by his Grandfather Jonathan, one of the last of the old Mississippi gamblers. The old man had worked the side-wheelers from St. Louis to New Orleans, and Durell's boyhood had been spent in the hot, green silences of the bayous around Peche Rouge in the delta country. His accent no longer betrayed him, thanks to his years at Yale and the war and his tours with G-2, the old OSS, and more recently, the CIA. His work was dangerous, and he was a dangerous man. Caution was as much a part of him as breathing. He was objective, even about Deirdre, since the difference between the living and the dead in his business was often the difference between a cool objectivity and a moment's emotional carelessness.

He could conceive of no other future for himself than doing the work he had been trained to do and wanted to do. But the orders in his pocket removed him, without warning or thanks, from the silent war he had been fighting. An ugly war, without bugles, fought in the dark alleys of all the corners of the world. Fought relentlessly, without mercy, where death came with a knife or a sniper's bullet, or the strangling agony of a swift garotte.

S AM DURELL walked past the communications room and heard the regular clacking of the teletypes and the murmur of high-frequency radios; then the analysis and synthesis rooms, where electronic computers winked and hummed and glowed. Finally he entered an outer office with walls lined with charts and filing cabinets and from there he went into General Dickinson McFee's office.

There were no windows. An air conditioner worked quietly; the venting grate was high in the wall. The small, trim gray man sat behind his desk, waiting for him.

"Sit down, Sam, and let's not be formal. And we won't say good-by, either. Your orders are strictly for temporary duty."

"Where am I going?" Durell asked.

"You know better than to ask. Sit down, will you? You may keep smoking, if you like." The little general hated cigarettes, and it was an indication that he, too, was perturbed by Durell's sudden assignment away from

K Section. "You can read your orders any time now."

"I haven't opened them yet."

"Read them here and then burn them."

It was an order. Durell nodded and slit the envelope and looked at the typewritten lines. He felt puzzled.

McFee said: "You report to the Waggonner Building."

"You knew that much, sir?"

"And that's all I know, Sam."

"It doesn't say where, in the Waggonner Building." Durell frowned. "What do I do, stand around the lobby until a girl with a rose in her teeth slinks up and asks me to buy her a sloe gin fizz?"

McFee shrugged. "Go there and see. When are you due?"

"Twenty minutes." Durell tore the order sheet and envelope into small strips, went to the opposite wall and opened a small iron door and dropped the bits of paper into the incinerator chute. He remained standing. "Was there anything else, General?"

"Just a word of advice. I have an idea where you are going and what you're to do. But you'll find out for yourself. If I'm right, I'd suggest extreme care. I don't have to emphasize how many police and intelligence arms the government has. Some are jealous of the others and spend more time competing with each other than in doing the job they're supposed to do. It's the penalty of governmental size, I suppose. The people you're going to work for are above inter-departmental rivalries, however. They once took Harry Keaton from us. Remember him?"

"Nobody has seen him since," Durell said flatly.

"Right. I think Harry is dead. He goofed it."

"You're quite cheerful," Durell said.

"I hate to lend you to them. I just hope you'll do better than Harry. You're the best I have, Sam, and there's been too much spent in training you, in spite of your Cajun attitudes, to make it easy to lose you." McFee stood up and they shook hands. "Take one of our cabs, the second at the corner. I left it for you. The driver knows where to drop you. You'll have five minutes to spare."

THE Waggonner Building was nondescript and ordinary, off Fourteenth Street in downtown Washington. It was two in the afternoon, and the lunch-hour

20

rush of government clerks had ebbed. The August heat was crushing, a humid blanket that smothered the city. Durell rather enjoyed the heat, since it reminded him of the bayou country.

The building had a false façade of marble, with a cigar stand beside the lobby doors, a bar to the left, with red neon signs advertising beer, a men's haberdashery and a cutlery shop with windows opening on the lobby area. Durell considered the business directory, but saw no familiar names. People moved all around him, but there were no familiar faces, either. The clock over the elevators read two minutes past two when he walked to the cigar stand and bought fresh cigarettes.

The woman attendant was middle-aged and looked tired, until her eyes met Durell's; then he saw a bright, amused intelligence in her glance.

"Waiting for someone?" she asked.

"Just waiting."

"Anything special?"

"Like a street car," Durell said.

"I see, sir. You might find one up on the fifth floor."

"Thank you."

"McGuire, Sloan and Levy. Room Five-fifty-four."

"Attorneys?"

"No, sir. Uniform manufacturers."

He took the elevator up. The corridor was dusty, lined with frosted-glass office doors. A fire escape stood open at the back and Durell walked there first, looked out at rooftops behind Fourteenth Street, and went back to Room 554. He knocked and walked in.

A blonde behind a typewriter took off harlequin glasses glittering with rhinestones and said: "Go right in. You are expected."

"Why all the hocus-pocus, Mata Hari?" he asked.

She stiffened. "I beg your pardon?"

He didn't bother to reply. An inner door opened into an office crowded with two shabby desks, a clothing rack loaded with samples of army and air force uniforms, and two men who turned to consider him. One wore a seersucker suit and looked thin and rumpled; his bald head glistened with perspiration. The second man had a young face that contrasted oddly with his snow-white hair. Durell closed the door behind him.

"Make yourself comfortable, Mr. Durell," said the white-haired man. "We do not operate on formal levels

21

here." He had the stamp of the military on him, but Durell did not know him or the older, bald man. "We appreciate your coming here."

"Did I have a choice?" Durell asked.

"You could have refused, of course. But then McFee would have had to let you go. McFee said you wouldn't like this, because your speciality has been working on overseas assignments. Our outfit has somewhat different problems. K Section deals primarily with espionage and counter-efforts concerned with defeating your opposite numbers abroad. Our viewpoint is much wider. Our problems, necessarily, are not as clear-cut as those you have been accustomed to consider. You might call us troubleshooters on a general scale, Mr. Durell."

"Odd balls," said the bald man. "Relax, Durell."

There was an air of command in these two men that was immediately felt. Durell sat down. He lit a cigarette and waited. The white-haired man smiled. "I'm Daniel Kincaid. This is John Wittington."

Neither man offered to shake hands.

Kincaid said: "Just to brief you a bit, you've been elected to a rather exclusive club. You may refer to us as the Special Bureau. Our staff is small and select. We are responsible to only two men, whom I shall not name. Mr. Wittington is second in command. You will probably never know our immediate superior, or the two men he reports to, but I can tell you we are associated with the National Planning Board and several other commissions that are not publicized. If you make any guesses about us, don't make them aloud, please."

Wittington cleared his throat, rubbed his bald head, and grunted. "I told you, odd balls. We get the strange ones. We use the FBI, the Treasury men, your own people from State, and G-2. A kind of clearing house for off-beat problems affecting our national security. From inside as well as out. The Reds are our biggest problem, but not our only headache. We do anything, like spotting a town where gambling elements or crooked unions tend to undermine our democratic way of life if their illegal powers reach up too far." The bald man looked annoyed. "Am I making a speech? I never can tell this without sounding like an orator on the Fourth of July."

"I think I understand," Durell said.

"We can collapse from weakness within as well as from enemy pressure on the outside. You people take care of the overt threats. We look into the others. Most of them do not constitute clear problems. We take a hint here and there and try to extrapolate what it may mean in terms of next year, or five or twenty years from now. Then we try to guide the matter the way it should go to insure our national safety. The first law of nature is to survive, but there is also the question of the conditions under which we survive. Are you still with me?"

Durell nodded. "Yes."

"You look troubled."

"I never heard of you people before."

"And you will forget us the moment this is over," Wittington snapped. "*If* you get the job. That depends. As I said, we sit on top of the other police agencies; we use their files and occasionally their men. For example, five years ago we correlated certain Foreign Service data and made some guesses and ran them through our machines." Wittington rubbed his bald head and grimaced. "I hate those mechanical monsters. Calculators, just gadgets without souls. We feed data to our beast, Lucy, and Lucy comes up with a prediction of what may happen. Five years ago, Lucy predicted atomic war in ten months, unless we did something about it. So we did it. And there was no war. Perhaps it proves nothing but the sound and fury in which we live today. I mean, Lucy might not have had proper data for an accurate prediction in the first place. But we took steps based on her forecast, and it worked out. She gave us another forecast recently that doesn't make much sense to those who have seen it. We're not sure what steps to take, if any. It's been decided we need more information to make a proper prediction; and you are the man to get that information for us. It depends, in part, upon your memory, Durell."

"My memory?"

"About Metzdorf."

"I was there in 1945," Durell said. "I was a captain in G-2 then, working with Amgot and the War Records Commission and the dismantling of the Ruhr industries, before that policy was reversed."

"The exact dates on Metzdorf?"

"I was there from June 10, 1945 to August 2, same year."

"Erich Corbin?" Wittington snapped.

Durell thought a moment. "Nothing there."

"Never heard of him?"

"No."

"Metzdorf Chemicals?"

"We stripped that plant; took the files and shipped them to Washington. The job was completed by the second week in July."

"Lieutenant Mark Fleming?"

The image of a baby-faced young man with a temperament like stone came to Durell. "He ran the packing and shipping detail."

"Thomas G. Everett?"

Durell shook his head. "Nothing there, either."

"Pete Labouisse?"

Durell crushed out his cigarette. "There is a family by that name in Bayou Peche Rouge. I come from there. Delta country, below New Orleans. I don't remember Pete. Or Pierre, as he was probably called. Just the family name is familiar."

"All right. Relax a minute."

WITTINGTON got up abruptly and went out through a back door, followed by Kincaid. Durell listened to the clacking of the typewriter in the outer room. Two minutes went by before Kincaid returned. He was alone. Wittington did not come back again.

Kincaid placed a folder on the battered desk and smiled briefly. "Your memory is fine. Mr. Wittington is quite satisfied."

"I'm in the club?"

"For this job, yes." Kincaid opened the file, frowned at it, and closed it. "As Mr. Wittington explained, our job is to gather data from various sources and synthesize them, if we can, into a pattern of meaning for the future. We deal in possibilities and probablities, in permutations and combinations. By now, I assume you understand that we chose you because, first, you were in Metzdorf in 1945, and second, you were in G-2 assigned to the collection of war records and supervising the dismantlement of the Nazi industrial strength. Are you sure you don't remember Herr Erich Corbin?"

"I never met him or heard of him."

Kincaid nodded. "He was plant supervisor for the Metzdorf Chemical Works. Absolutely nonpolitical, as far as every record goes. Neither nazi nor communist, socialist or democrat, fish or fowl."

"How did he keep his job?"

"He was good. A genius, of sorts. He guided the development of such drugs as scopolomine for espionage usage and experiments in their concentration camps. And nerve gases of various sorts. Very good technician. Fine administrator. He'll be fifty-one years of age now."

"Then he's still alive?"

"Oh, yes. He went to Berlin after the war and wandered over to East Germany and dropped out of sight for all these years. Worked for the Russians, but don't get ideas about that. As I said, he is totally apolitical. He believes too strongly in the right of the individual to a profit, you see, and freedom of enterprise. The criminal mind has no sympathy for a totalitarian police state."

"Why do you say Herr Corbin is a criminal?"

"His record is here. Embezzlement, as a young clerk with a shipping concern in Hamburg. A scrape with the Weimar Republic police, for smuggling heroin. He was perfectly spotted for drug traffic, with his merchant marine connections and then his job in the chemical works, which gave him access to drug supplies merely by juggling the books. In his late thirties he presumably reformed and became the respectable supervisor of the chemical division of the Metzdorf Works. Here is a picture of him. You can't keep it, of course. Take a good look and memorize it."

Durell studied the glossy print Kincaid handed him. He noted the round forehead, the thinning grayish hair, the sharp nose, the cold Teutonic eyes behind rimless spectacles. His glance absorbed the physical description: height five four, weight 162, eyes gray, hair gray, no distinguishing scars. He ignored the fingerprints in the ruled boxes below the print and handed back the photo. Kincaid took a pipe from his pocket and filled it awkwardly, spilling tobacco crumbs on the desk top.

"Erich Corbin," Kincaid said, "came to the U.S. almost a year ago, in September, on a visiting-alien permit. Your office and the FBI had no reason to deny him entry. Ostensibly, he came over to inspect some pharmaceutical plants in New Jersey; and he did, for two months. The FBI kept him under surveillance, just to be on the safe side."

Kincaid paused. "Corbin came here with a wife, by the way. Newlyweds. An American girl who had been

25

living abroad since 1949, until she married Erich in West Berlin. Jessica Handley, maiden name, age twenty-eight right now. Graduated Des Moines, dramatic student. Came from Fremont, Iowa—a farm girl. Lived in Greenwich Village for a time, made an unsuccessful stab at a theatrical career, and then went over to Paris."

"What did she do there?"

"We don't know," Kincaid said simply.

"Do you have her picture, too?"

"Passport, only." Kincaid slid another enlargement over the desk. Durell noted the blonde girl's sulky mouth, the look of harsh wisdom in her pale eyes. Kincaid said: "Her story, told frankly, is that she lived by sponging on American tourists over there. We think she was the mistress of a Swiss exporter named Krell, for a time; and we're sure she was the mistress of a young Yugoslav attache at their Paris embassy. Anyway, she returned to the States as Herr Erich Corbin's wife."

"Where are they now?" Durell asked.

"Missing. They vanished two days before last Christmas—and that's item one in the picture." Kincaid struck two matches for his pipe, puffed futilely, and put it down. "The FBI files that came to us in a purely routine way indicated one interesting thing. Corbin's wife, Jessie, deliberately sought out and made the acquaintance of Lieutenant Mark Fleming, in a New York nightclub. The FBI has Fleming on their criminal list. The man had a good army record, but a lot of gun-happy characters were just what the army needed in those days. Actually, Fleming's record is that of a small-time hoodlum since boyhood, and he went right back to his old life when he mustered out. Fleming dropped out of sight, by the way, the same time the Corbins disappeared; and that's the second interesting item."

"Fleming was in charge of the detail that removed the files from the Metzdorf plant," Durell said.

"Right. Of course, this didn't have much importance to our analysts until the third factor was presented. It came from the War Department—again, a routine memorandum. Certain records in their storage warehouse across the Potomac have been tampered with. It happened three months ago. Nothing apparently stolen. Just pawed around. Among them were the cartons of records from the Metzdorf plant."

"Haven't they been analyzed and returned by now?"

Kincaid spread his neat hands. "You know how it goes. The army sent home shiploads of the stuff. Then it put only a handful of clerks to sorting and recording all those tons of paper. Even after all these years, the Metzdorf files were undisturbed, just as they had been placed in storage pending a check."

Durell grinned. "I remember those men sweated plenty, getting those heavy cases down into the trucks."

"But you don't remember a Thomas Everett?"

"No," Durell said.

"Well, no real reason why you should." Kincaid tapped the pipe stem against his white teeth. It was quiet in the office. "Anyway, one of our men happened to be diddling with this data and connected Corbin with the disturbed Metzdorf files. We sent him over to double-check. There was a boxful of formulas, most of them known to our chemical men; and some incomplete and useless experimental work." Kincaid sighed. Durell looked at his white hair and wondered how it had happened, with his young face. "Well, you heard what Mr. Wittington thinks of our prediction machine. He doesn't trust it. He prefers instinct, hunches—anything. He sent over to the army for the service records of the men who moved the files from the Metzdorf Works, and we got their names. That's how we ran across your name, too. Mr. Wittington thinks there is some rather nasty meaning in the fact that Herr Corbin came to the United States and picked up contact with ex-Lieutenant Fleming—a man with a vicious criminal mind—and then they all vanished after the storage files were tampered with."

"Has Mr. Wittington come up with any suppositions?"

"Not yet. But since Corbin contacted Fleming, we checked the other members of that squad. Ten days ago we learned about Tom Everett, a former Pfc in the squad, a gas station owner out in Arizona. He was found by his wife. Very dead, with his throat cut."

"Ten days ago?"

"Cold trail. Nothing there. Could be coincidence, but we don't buy it. Everett was murdered then, and we've had two other reports since. A second man in the squad, John Miller, was killed Tuesday a week since. Same method. A knife across the throat. And a Perry Hayward, a Madison Avenue huckster, but a nice chap with the usual wife, four kids, and a mortgaged home in West-

27

port, Connecticut. Found in the men's room at Grand Central, in one of the lavatory booths. Same method."

"Then there are only two left," Durell said. "A Sergeant Slago. I remember him. And you mentioned Pete Labouisse."

Kincaid tried to light his pipe again. "We can't find Slago. Maybe he's with Fleming; or maybe he's dead. He was a merchant seaman for a time, but there're no recent records of him in Department of Commerce, the Maritime Commission, or the seamen's union."

"Does your Mr. Wittington know why these men were killed?"

Kincaid shook his head. "Only that something connects these men with Corbin's arrival in this country. We don't think it's some military secret the Communists want. Forget your work with the CIA, Durell. As Mr. Wittington says, we get the odd-ball cases. We're thinking along lines of criminal endeavor. We want more facts so we can estimate the potential in this matter. Perhaps it will turn out to be unimportant to us. In that case, we simply turn it all over to the FBI."

Durell stood up. "And I'm to get those facts?"

Kincaid looked at him. "You're to find Erich Corbin. Not to interfere with him, please. Just find him."

"And Labouisse?"

"Another reason you were picked. The last survivor, barring Slago. He comes from your home parish. Go home on vacation and see-him."

"Has he been warned or contacted yet?"

"He's been out to sea on a shrimp boat, due back tomorrow. The boat is the *Deux Soeurs*. See if he has anything Corbin might be looking for. And—"

Durell waited.

"Try to keep his head on his shoulders, eh?"

Chapter Three

MARK drew the razor carelessly down the side of his face. The blade nicked his skin and he started and tossed the razor down into the bowl. His hands

28

were shaking, and he told himself it had to stop. He felt anger, and that was good, and he drew a steadying breath, feeling the tremor in his arms as he leaned on the washbowl, head down.

It was the heat, he told himself, that was all. This damned bayou country, where the air was like breathing water, drowning you. But it wouldn't last long. They were near the end of the line.

New York had been a mess. The job with Perry Hayward had been his, since Slago was not the sort to approach Perry's advertising office. It was easy enough to begin, but Perry was downright cool and suspicious from the start. He had always been a snobbish bastard. College punk in gray flannels, even in the summer heat. Clean and rich-looking, talking with a Harvard accent, just as phony as he had been in Germany. Perry resented him because he had a lieutenant's bars then. Mark's first few questions had seemed to alert him, and for a few moments Mark had begun to hope that their search was at an end. But he hadn't gotten anywhere. He denied ever seeing the advertisement asking for war souvenirs in the form of Hitler autographs or letters, and he didn't even remember the detail, although he remembered Metzdorf. He hadn't been lying, either.

Mark grinned at his reflection in the bath mirror. That sort didn't lie with a knife at his throat. Good thing Slago had joined them in the lavatory down in Grand Central. Hell of a place to slice a guy's throat. There had been a bad moment with that drunk suddenly wanting to get into the booth, and when the blood that had missed the bowl went splashing bright red and thick on the tiled floor behind the swinging door, while men came and went all around them. A hell of a bad moment.

Mark dried his face and went into the bedroom he shared with Slago. This was the worst of the places they had stayed in—a cheap fishing camp named Moon's, two miles up the highway from Bayou Peche Rouge. The heat made him sick to his stomach, and he had had only coffee all day. And that was loaded with the chicory that Louisianans liked.

Slago was sprawled on Mark's bed, muddy shoes staining the cheap cover. The sight of the barrel-chested man with his cropped salt-and-pepper hair instilled a sudden fury in Mark.

"Get your goddam feet off my bed," he snapped.

Slago opened his mean, small eyes. He stared at Mark in silence, then said: "You ain't a lieutenant any more, buddy boy."

"I still give orders. Move your feet."

"The Dutchman gives orders, not you." Slago grinned slowly. "And you know something, Mark? Nobody would miss you in this operation. All you done is drive that big Cad like you owned it. And you don't own it. It's Corbin's." Something in Mark's face made Slago's rumbling voice end. He grinned and lifted his feet off the bed and looked at the pinch bottle on the floor. "You're just getting nervous, buddy boy."

Mark sat down on the edge of the bed and picked up the bottle. He knew that in this heat he ought not to drink, but he swallowed heavily, feeling the Scotch glow in the pit of his stomach. He saw Slago watching him with a curiously wary expression in his eyes.

"Listen," Mark said. "What do you really think about Corbin?"

"He's nuts," Slago said flatly. "But why worry? He's got dough, right? And we'll get it, sooner or later."

"We didn't start this just for peanuts. And I keep thinking about this thing we're after. Maybe one of the three we finished had it. We know it hasn't been lost or burned up, because of that A. Greene who answered the ad and then dropped it. But maybe one of the three—suppose we killed them too soon?"

Slago laughed. "You'd like one of them to have told the cops what we asked about and blow the whole thing sky high? We decided, didn't we? Nobody left behind to talk about it. Who's going to remember they were all in the same squad? Some hick sheriff in Arizona? Or some fat chief of police in Indiana? Hell, Mark, take it easy. Labouisse has it. He's the last."

"Is he?" Mark asked. Slago didn't say anything. Mark added softly: "There's you and me, Slago."

It grew very quiet in the cabin. Mark waited, and then knew he had waited too long. Suspicion flickered in Slago's little eyes. From outside came the racket of an outboard motor on the little river that moved sluggishly into Bayou Peche Rouge. The distant thumping of a juke box in Moon's bar came across the fishing camp. A girl giggled in one of the cabins. It was growing dark. There were deep shadows in the room.

30

Slago said mildly: "I think we're all crazy, buddy boy."

"Maybe so. But if Labouisse doesn't have it, there's only you and me. I know *I* don't have it. But I don't know about you."

"Watch your mouth," Slago said.

"You think I'd be stupid enough to let this go on, if I had Erich's papers?" Mark snapped. "Listen, I want that thing for Corbin. We get nowhere without it. He needs it. After that, we get into any bank in the country, like walking in and helping ourselves and walking out again. Nobody knows, nobody remembers. All the money we want. I'm not going to stand still if you're playing some stupid game with me."

Slago took out his switchblade, snapped it open, and began cleaning his fingernails. "You always had too much brains for your own good. Always figuring odds and percentages, buddy boy. You get sick in the head that way. Don't worry about the guys I killed. They're just crumbs," Slago said quietly.

Mark considered the bottle. His stomach was upset, and he didn't drink any more. "Labouisse has it, then. If he didn't burn it or lose it or sell it to somebody else for a souvenir aften we advertised."

"He has it," Slago agreed. "And when we get it, we all live in clover down in South America." The tension was gone from the room. "I'd like that plenty," Slago said softly. "I hear them Spanish women are like red peppers, especially when they're young. I'd like to bite off some of that."

Mark got up off the bed and pushed open the screen door and let it whine and slam behind him. The shabby green shades in Corbin's cabin were drawn, and he heard the sound of a shower running. He walked over to Corbin's door and knocked and walked in.

THIS cabin was identical with the one he shared with Slago, but it was neat and tidy, not strewn with clothes the way Slago lived, like a pig. Erich was not in sight. The bathroom door was partly open for air, and the hiss of the shower came from there. Mark closed the outer door quietly. The outboard motor on the river was gone. Neon lights winked over the fisherman's camp, in the fly-specked window of the bar where beer, sandwiches, Coke and fishing tackle were for sale to the sportsmen. Darkness had come, and insects and heat were more oppressive than before. The heat was almost tangible, like something you could push and claw at.

"Erich? Jessie?"

He walked deliberately into the bath, the beat of his heart suddenly quickening. He saw her just as she stepped out of the tin shower cabinet. Long clean legs, womanly hips, high proud breasts, jeweled with the tepid water she had just turned off. She had tied a towel around her long hair. Mark heard the sudden thud of his pulse in his ears. He didn't move, and she didn't try to cover her nakedness. Her violet eyes went cautious and then blank.

"Don't be foolish, Mark," she said softly. "Get out."

"I'm not worried about anything. Are you?"

"Erich will be back soon. Stop staring at me. Didn't you ever see a woman before?"

"Not like you, Jessie." His voice tricked him, suddenly going hoarse with the uneven stroke of his heart. "You're beautiful."

"Hand me that towel," she said calmly.

He shook his head. "Get it yourself. I like to see you move around."

She shook her head impatiently and reached for the bath towel on the rack. He let her get her hand on it before he caught her wirst and pulled her roughly to him. For just a moment she fought against his solid strength, and then she stumbled against him and caught at his shoulder. His hands slid over her wet body.

"Don't, Mark."

"You promised me," he whispered.

"I never."

"The way you looked at me."

"No."

"What's Erich to you? An old man. You don't love him. Why did you ever hook up with him, anyway?"

"He brought me back, Mark."

"Is that all? Is that why you married him?"

"That's one of the reasons."

"But you don't love him. And I'm crazy about you, Jessie."

He forced her head up, cupping his hand under her chin, and made her meet his eyes. In the gathering dusk, her violet eyes seemed enormous, swimming darkly, and then they suddenly went blank again with that opacity

32

he could not understand. It was as if she retreated somewhere he could not follow. To hell with her mind, he
thought savagely. His blood pounded in him. His hands
moved and he felt her slowly gathering response; he
heard the whispered exhalation of her breath and her
weight clung more heavily. They moved together through
the doorway toward the bed. Her head was down, and
he could not see the expression on her face. The room
was dark and hot and filled with the small sounds they
made.

He didn't hear the door slam until it was too late.

Jessie slapped him. He hardly felt it. Her gesture
was too late to hide the obvious position of surrender
she had adopted.

Erich stood for a moment inside the doorway. He was
a small man, but in Mark's eyes he loomed as an enormous shadow against the irregular pulse of red neon
light from Moon's bar across the parking lot. The woman
in the cabin at the end of the row giggled again. A
bottle broke somewhere. A bird called, forlornly.

Erich had a Luger in his hand.

Mark got off the bed slowly, adjusting himself. His
voice sounded distant to him. "Wait a minute, Erich.
You don't understand."

"But I do," Corbin said gently. "Even in this country,
I could kill you with justice. Jessie, please get dressed.
Quickly, now. And do not come out until I call you."

"Erich, don't do anything silly." She sounded cold
and sure of herself. "Remember what we planned."

"I remember everything, *liebchen*. Everything I know
about you. Go and do as I say. I will not kill him. We
are almost at the end of our first phase of the plan.
Would I risk disaster by firing a gun in this place, when
we are so near success? I am not so stupid."

Mark said flatly: "Then put away the gun."

"You understand, I let you go because of necessity.
And because I know nothing happened, because you had
not the time. But I shall not forget." Corbin's glasses
winked suddenly as he turned his head to watch Jessie's
pale body move obediently into the bathroom. Then he
looked back at Mark. "Go call Sergeant Slago. I have
located our man. He is not a shrimp fisherman, after
all. It is only a part-time occupation with him. The boat
met with an unexpected gale and put in at a port twenty
miles from here. He is still there. I telephoned. We will

33

meet him there. You and Slago must be very careful, very sure this time. He has it. We must operate on the assumption that he is the man named A. Greene who answered our advertisement, and then vanished. When we get what we want, I shall have to work quietly for a day or two, preparing what we need. I would appreciate it if you did not disturb me by making further advances toward my wife."

There was a fanatical quality in Corbin's voice that brooked no further argument. Mark was acutely aware of the sounds of Jessie's movements in the bath. He nodded. He was covered with sticky perspiration. His stomach burned with indigestion. Anyone else, with a wife like Jessie, finding her like this, would have blown his cork.

He paused outside and looked at his watch. It was eight-thirty. His body ached with frustration. Slowly, he walked across the parking lot toward the bar for another drink.

Chapter Four

D URELL arrived in New Orleans at nine o'clock the next morning. He rented a black Chevrolet at the airport, had breakfast at the counter, and drove south into the delta country. The heat was oppressive, but he did not mind it. He wore a thinly woven sport shirt with an open collar, light gabardine slacks, and buckled sandals. His .38, a Smith & Wesson with a very short barrel, was in his brown pigskin suitcase.

He was in Bayou Peche Rouge at ten and had coffee with his grandfather Jonathan aboard the hulk of the *Three Belles*. The old man was unchanged, no different since Durell's boyhood. He was tall and straight, with thick white hair and alert blue eyes, and in the back of his mind, ready for instant use, lay every clean and dirty trick of the gambling trade. He had won the ancient Mississippi sidewheeler on the turn of a card and then, on learning that his wife had died in the fire that gutted the house on the bayou, he had run the old steamboat

34

up into the mud beside the fire-blackened chimneys and charred walls, and he had lived there ever since. The sidewheeler itself had burned to the waterline once, but he had stubbornly rebuilt her. Durell had no idea how much the old man was worth. Jonathan had raised him after an accident took both Sam's parents, and the vast, echoing hull of the steamboat, with its dusty and faded Victorian splendors, was the only home he had ever recognized.

They did not talk about Durell's business until after they'd had their coffee. The old man's voice was firm. "You look fine, Samuel, just fine." They stood in the high pilothouse of the steamboat, forward of the twin, rusty smokestacks. The old man wore a captain's visored cap on his white hair. "It's good to see you again, son."

"And good to see you, Grandpa." Durell had called Jonathan from Washington. "Did you find out anything about Labouisse?"

The old man grinned. "He's engaged to marry a former lady love of yours. Samuel. Remember Angelina, boy?"

Durell smiled briefly. "I remember."

"A young colt must get his studding done early. You think I didn't know how you took her that day?"

"You were always a step ahead of me, Grandpa." Durell had a quick memory of a sultry day in the green stillness of the bayous. He recalled the way the swamp grass had felt on the old *cheniere* where he had awkwardly fumbled through his first attempt at love.

"She's grown up into a mighty handsome woman, Samuel."

"What about Pierre?"

"He didn't come home last night from his fishing trip," Jonathan said. "Nobody has heard from him yet." The old man's glance was acute. "I know the work you do, Samuel. But I can't figure out what a simple man like Pete Labouisse could have to do with your job."

"He has something the government is looking for."

"Pete?" Jonathan made a snickering sound. "He's missing the proverbial pot, boy. Set himself up as a photographer in Peche Rouge, studio and all, takin' baby pictures of the Cajun women's set. Don't make much of a livin' at it, so he goes mate on Joe Tibault's shrimper out on the Gulf, now and then. Reckon when he marries Angelina, though, he'll move into the general store and be fixed good in more ways than one. That Angelina is a woman, Samuel. What could Pete have that Washington wants?"

"We're not sure yet. And it's not just Washington," Durell said. "Somebody else wants it. If they get to him first, Pierre will suddenly find that somebody has cut his throat." The old man looked sober for a long moment. Durell felt a great wave of affection for him. He said: "I stopped at the Town Landing, Grandpa, but Joe Tibault's boat wasn't there. Where is he?"

"Ran into bad weather out in the Gulf. Knocked out their radio and damaged the engine. They put in a ways down the shore yesterday, late in the evening. I saw Angelina last night, after you called. She hadn't heard from Pete, so I drove down. Joe says a man was waiting for Pete and they drove off in this fancy car."

"If Pete hasn't come home, then I may have got here too late," Durell said.

"It still don't figure that Labouisse has anything of value to anybody. Except maybe to Angelina." The old man laughed again. "Make me twenty years younger, and I'd relish the job of consoling her."

"You'd be plenty man for her, Grandpa." Durell grinned. "Wasn't Pete given up for drowned some months ago when he went shrimping and the boat was lost? Joe Tibault told me something about it."

Jonathan nodded. "Everybody in Peche Rouge figured Pete had gone to the bottom. Turned out he drifted around on some wreckage and was picked up by some Mexicans operating out of Yucatan. Pete didn't figure anybody would miss him much, so he stayed there for a spell. Angelina already had a lawyer goin' through Pete's effects, ready to sell off his camera equipment and stuff. But Pete showed up in time to keep her from sellin' his shirt. Gave her a black eye for not havin' faith in his return." The old man smiled wryly. "Where you going, Samuel?"

Durell had stood up. "I'd better talk to Angelina."

"She remembers you well, son."

"Maybe I'm too late in more ways than one," Durell replied.

H E HAD parked the rented Chevy in the shade of the fire-blackened ruins in the clearing opposite the sidewheeler's mooring. Vegetation had long ago softened the tragic outlines of the gutted house. A fish jumped and splashed in the black-green waters of the bayou behind him. A graveled lane led to the Peche Rouge road, and he drove slowly through the humid morning mist that shrouded the moss-draped live oaks and gaunt cypress trees on either side of the bayou.

The town was small, with the highway acting as the main street. There were the usual bars and diner, the National Bank in traditional granite, a courthouse square with more giant oaks, two sporting-goods shops, and the general store that Angelina had inherited from her father, Abner Greene. Durell drove slowly by each place as it evoked his boyhood memories. The old frame school building had been replaced by one of brick, with coldly functional lines that jarred radically with the sleepy, weatherbeaten houses surrounding it. There were the same churches, however, and the Town Landing on the bayou canal looked drowned in golden sunlight. Pelicans swam in dirty-brown awkwardness in the murky waters around the boats tied to the pier. At the northern edge of the town limits he found Pete Labouisse's photo shop.

It was in a gray, two-story frame house, in the front of which had been placed a store window. The house needed a coat of paint. The scrubby lawn beyond the sagging picket fence needed mowing. There was a scanty display of photographic equipment, cameras and enlargers, but most of the window space was filled with big yellow and red Kodak ads. Behind the display, a large black window shade had been drawn against the heat of the morning sun.

Nobody was in sight. Durell drove a bit farther and parked in front of a diner and walked back. The heat clamped on the back of his neck like a giant fist. Distantly, from the center of town, came the sound of church bells. Even the insects were somnolent in the humidity.

There were framed baby portraits, none of them very good technically, flanking the front door. Durell did not go in through the gate in the picket fence. He cut between the next two houses and returned to the back of the building by way of a sandy lane edged with a rickety board fence. Weeds grew chest-high on either side of the walk. Behind the house was a wilderness of scrub pine that merged into the richer green of the bayou, and he realized that the channel was not too far off when he heard the steady beat of a boat's motor through the trees.

The upper windows were closed with wooden shutters. A gallery circled the back end of the house, with a separate flight of steps going up to a door on the second level. A pirogue rested on two sawhorses among the weeds in the back yard.

Durell felt the weight of his gun in its holster under his arm. He had put on his jacket in order to cover the revolver, and he felt a trickle of perspiration sliding down his chest as he paused in the shadows of the fence. He didn't like the desolate air of this place. He had approached danger many times before, and he had developed an intuitive feeling for it, much like the sixth sense Jonathan had instilled in him toward a poker hand. In his business a hunch was usually worthless, inferior to an objective appraisal of a given situation, with a logical course of action worked out beforehand. Yet his feeling of danger persisted, and he did not deny its importance.

He waited and watched, but he saw nothing and heard nothing except the occasional sound of traffic on the highway beyond the house. Finally he left the shadows of the fence and walked around the pirogue in the back yard and approached the back door. It was standing slightly open.

He tested the board steps going up to it. They would creak under his weight, and he walked on the very edge, moving without sound until he touched the weathered door panel. Insects clicked and hummed and buzzed in the weeds behind him. The passing boat in the invisible canal had gone by. A fish-hawk sailed silently overhead and settled in one of the Australian pines. Durell pushed the door open, moving close inside with the swing of it as he had been trained to do, and then slid quickly to one side against the wall.

Something fell over with a loud, echoing clatter. He got his gun in his hand, ready for use. But nothing more happened.

He saw that a tin pail had been balanced precariously on the board floor just inside the doorway, and he knew it had been set there deliberately, to give warning to someone inside the house if the door should be

38

opened. Pressure began to exert itself along his nerves. Pete Labouisse was the last survivor of the squad, except for Fleming and Slago. Perhaps he wasn't too late, after all.

He found himself in an old-fashioned, summer kitchen, a shed filled with odds and ends of broken furniture, lumber, and what looked like the parts of a copper still. Another door was open directly ahead. He waited, listening, then moved through this doorway into a more modern kitchen, and then he waited again.

A board creaked faintly in the ceiling overhead.

Durell moved into the corridor. To his right was an open door with a small printed sign thumbtacked to it: *Darkroom.* He glimpsed wash trays, shelves of chemical bottles, two enlargers on a metal-topped table. A third enlarger lay on the floor, shattered, where it had been carelessly or irritably shoved off the worktable. A filing cabinet stood open, and small yellow envelopes of negatives were scattered on the linoleum floor. The air was heavy with the sharp smell of spilled developing solutions.

The floor board upstairs creaked again.

Durell drifted silently toward the front of the house. There was no one in the front shop, but a glimpse of wreckage and supplies strewn about behind the glass-topped counters showed that this too, had been searched with quick impatience. He turned his body slightly and looked up the shadowy stairway to the second-floor landing.

With every window in the house shuttered, the place was a dark oven, filled with the smell of mildew that not even the pungency of spilled photographic acids could cover. A truck rumbled by on the highway, and windowpanes rattled everywhere. Whoever was upstairs took advantage of the sound to retreat a few cautious steps toward the back gallery. Whoever it was, he was trying to circle around toward the back door on that gallery and get down the rear stairway while Durell was still in the front part of the house.

Durell went up the steps with a quick, silent rush.

A shadow lunged to the left and away from him in the hallway. Something hurtled through the air and missed his head and crashed with the sound of splintering glass against the wall at his side.

"Hold it," Durell called softly. "You're covered."

H E GLIMPSED an oval face, a flash of white, and then the shadow plunged toward the back door. Durell lifted his gun, then suddenly tossed it aside and dived for the figure. It was a girl. She gasped in sudden terror and whirled, fighting him, her nails scratching at his face, her knee rising expertly to disable him. He slipped by her attack and caught one arm and forced it firmly up behind her back, driving her a few stumbling steps ahead of him until she jolted against the corridor wall.

"Take it easy," he said gently.

"Let me go!" she breathed. "You filthy, thieving murderer—"

She was full and firm, writhing in his grip. She wore a man's chambrey shirt and skin-tight dungarees. Her long black hair swung wildly across Durell's face as she tried to bend her neck and bite at his hands. Durell locked an ankle across hers and threw her off balance. She fell to the floor, dragging him with her.

"Easy, Angelina," he said.

She struggled another instant, arching her body to throw off his weight. Then she abruptly went limp and silent, except for the quick panting of her breath. "Who are you?" she whispered.

"Durell." He laughed softly. "Sam Durell. Are you alone here, Angelina?"

He saw the widening shine of her dark eyes. Her face moved. "What?"

"Is anyone else in the house?"

"No, no." Her voice was small. "Sam?"

"That's right."

"Let me look at you."

He released her cautiously. Her body was quiet under him, except for the quick tumult of her breathing.

"Oh, God. Sam? Sam Durell? Is it really you?"

"Yes."

"Where did you—I haven't seen you in so long. And now you come back like this, scaring the life out of me—" She swallowed and pushed at her black hair with the back of her hand. "You're with the FBI, aren't you?"

"Not exactly."

"But you're a cop, aren't you? Your grandfather said—"

"Not exactly a cop."

"Let me up, Sam."

He stood up in the dim hallway. Light came through the shuttered door to the rear gallery, making bright yellow bars on the faded rose-colored carpet. Dust motes danced in the swirl of air currents when he moved. The girl stared up at him with slowly widening eyes.

She was lovely. She had the wild beauty of the dark bayous in her, with the raven night caught in her disheveled black hair. The depth of deep bayou pools was in her eyes. Her mouth was wide, her lower lip full and sensuous, trembling until she caught it between even white teeth. The buttons of her chambray shirt had broken loose and he saw the smooth curves of her unsupported breasts. He remembered her vividly as a girl, meeting him behind her father's store in Bayou Peche Rouge. How long ago since he had last seen her? Ten, twelve years? He remembered the awkward, exploratory nights they had shared. Their first experience, the first for either of them. He had never forgotten her. She had grown into a rich, dark beauty, like the wild orchids that bloomed in the green fastness of the delta swamps.

"Are you remembering, Sam?" she whispered.

"This isn't the time to remember anything," he said. "Where is Pierre?"

She rose gracefully to her feet. She was tall for a woman. "What brought you here just now, Sam?"

"I'm looking for Labouisse," Durell said flatly. "I came down from Washington to try to keep something from happening to him."

"You came too late. It's already happened."

"Did you search this place, Angelina?"

"No."

"Did you see who did it?"

"No."

"What were they looking for? Did Pete tell you?"

"I don't know. He can't talk. He—" She shook her head. In the gloom of the hallway, her face reflected deep terror. "I came back to get some things for him. To try to help him. And then I heard you come in. My heart almost stopped. It's still beating—so crazy— Sam, don't look at me like that. Please. Not now."

"Where is Pete?" he asked again.

"I'll take you to him," she said softly. "I know I can trust you. Some men caught him and did terrible things to him. He got away from them, though, and came through the swamps in a pirogue. I found him down in Petit Gauche Channel. Remember it?"

"I remember. Is he still there?"

"Come," she said. "I was just picking up some bandages. But I think I'm too late, anyway. I think he'll be dead when we get there."

Chapter Five

DURELL walked to the gallery door and looked out. The lane and the board fence and the swamps beyond were drowned in silent sunshine. He looked beyond the scrub pines that merged into the oak and cypress a little farther out. Nothing moved that he could see. But he did not expose himself to anyone who might be out there. He turned back as Angelina came toward him. Her hands were empty.

"Where are the first-aid supplies you came to get?"

"You didn't give me a chance to pick them up." Her hand was spread on her breast. "You frightened me so, Sam . . ."

"Get the stuff we'll need," he said briefly. "And stay away from this door. Don't go out until I join you." He saw her dark eyes go wide again. She understood their danger. "Which is Pete's bedroom?"

She pointed down the hall. "That one, I think."

"Don't you know?"

She smiled. "Yes, it's that one, Sam."

He left her and went into the bedroom. It had been ransacked like the rest of the house, but much more thoroughly than the shop and the darkroom below. Durell paused in the middle of the room. The air smelled dead behind the closed shutters. In the faint light that seeped through the slats, he saw that the bed had been torn apart, the mattress slewed to the floor, and every drawer in the huge mahogany dresser stood open, with Pete's clothing scattered everywhere. His glance settled on a foot locker that had been pulled from a corner and stood askew under the windows. The broken hasp on the lock showed how it had been forced open. Army uniforms, combat boots, and a helmet liner lay on the floor. A bag containing a Purple Heart medal and a

Bronze Star had been dumped without ceremony beside the helmet liner. A collection of snapshots had been given the same treatment. Durell picked up two or three. One of them showed Pete Labouisse in front of the cathedral at Chartres. A smiling, chunky G.I. with a broad face and heavy black brows and an air of excitement in the way he stood and looked into the sun and the camera. Another showed him with his arm around a Belgian farm girl, with a little boy standing to one side, looking frightened. Durell dropped the snapshots back on the floor. A black and silver crucifix shone on the wall over the bed. He looked at it for a moment and then returned to the trunk. A large manila envelope lay to one side, partly hidden under the tumbled uniforms. He opened it and saw copies of citations, service records, letters. One of the letters was on the stationery of the old Reichskanzelrei. It was signed by Goering. He leafed quickly through the sheaf of souvenirs. He didn't find what he was looking for; he hadn't really expected to.

Angelina appeared in the doorway, her figure magnificent in her chambray shirt and tight dungarees. "What is it, Sam?" She pushed again at her black hair on her forehead. She carried a small packet of surgical gauze, a bottle of iodine, a pair of scissors. "What are you looking for?"

"Don't you know?" he asked.

"I can't imagine. I don't know what this is all about."

"Are you sure of that?"

"Sam, don't make noises like a cop to me. This is Angelina, remember? My man has been hurt, and he needs help. I'm going back to him. Right now."

"All right. But be careful."

It was not far from the house on the highway. A path had been beaten through the swamp, twisting and turning among the tall cypress knees, winding deep into the green jungle of the bayou. The girl led the way. Durell walked quietly and alertly behind her. Now and then he watched the lithe movement of her hips in the tight denims she wore, and he remembered how it had been many years ago. He did not see the pirogue until Angelina halted suddenly.

"Over there," she whispered.

Black water gleamed through the underbrush. Far in the distance, on the main canal from Bayou Peche

Rouge, came the steady beat of a fishing boat's diesel. Insects hummed and flickered through the slanting shafts of sunlight that came down through the trees.

"Stay where you are," Durell told the girl.

He went ahead cautiously. In a moment he saw the pirogue, driven up into the mud between two towering cypress trees, almost hidden by a curtain of moss. At first he thought the pirogue was empty. Then he saw the man sprawled in the bottom of the boat, on his back, his face upturned to a narrow angle of sunlight that picked him out. Something went thrashing away through the brush as Durell approached. The flies and other insects were more reluctant to leave.

His glance flicked away from the pirogue to another boat tied to a pine stump at the water's edge. It was a small outboard runabout, painted dark green and white. Nobody was in it. A woman's white handbag lay on one of the seats.

He looked again at Pete Labouisse. Only in a general way did he resemble the young GI in the snapshots. He had become pudgy, and most of his dark hair was gone except for a curly fringe around the gleaming baldness in the middle of his scalp. His eyes stared unwinkingly into the spear of sunlight that touched his face, and Durell did not have to examine him to know that he was dead.

He moved closer, anyway. The dead man was wearing cowhide fishing boots, old denims, a thin checked work shirt almost colorless from many salt-water washings. His face was badly battered, and there was blood on each hand where his fingernails had been crushed, and there was blood on the dungarees between his legs. Durell let out his breath in a long sigh. His face was like stone as he stepped beside the pirogue and very carefully loosened the wide leather belt around the trousers and looked at the ugly wound between the dead man's legs. He tasted acid in his throat. He suddenly felt cold.

A quick, shuddering gasp came from behind him and he looked up and saw Angelina with both hands pressed hard across her mouth.

"Get away," he said harshly.

"But why—how could they—"

"Don't ask me. I told you to get away." Durell straightened and pushed her back toward the trail. Angelina stumbled and fell to her knees and covered her face with her hands. A moaning came from her. Durell said quickly: "Is that your runabout, with the pirogue?"

Her head moved, nodding. Her hair screened her face.

"How did you happen to find him here?" he insisted.

"I—I usually come to his house this way."

"And he was alive when you found him?"

"I thought he was, yes."

Durell was insistent. "Did he say anything to you at all? Did he say who did it?"

"N-no."

"Didn't you examine him when you found him?"

"I was—I didn't want to touch him."

The silent green of the underbrush and the dark waters of the swamp were suddenly and infinitely menacing. Durell still felt cold. "Go ahead and be sick, if you want to," he said gently.

She shook her head. "I'm all right now."

He helped her to her feet. Her weight was soft and heavy against him. "Sam, I don't understand. Why should anyone do such a horrible thing? What kind of men were they?"

"I don't know," he said. His voice was curiously flat. "I expect to find out."

H E HAD the feeling they were being watched. The way back to the house seemed shorter on the return than on going, and although he saw nothing out of the ordinary, the feeling that his every step was being observed remained with him. Angelina walked quietly beside him. Some of the shock was gone from her eyes, and he kept talking to her, questioning her, to help her mind with other problems.

"Were you in love with him, Angelina?"

"I don't know. Perhaps. What is love? He was a good man. He wanted me; he was in love with me for a long time." Her eyes slanted briefly up at Durell's lean face. "Nobody has ever had me since we—since you, Sam. Do you believe that?"

"Why not?" he said. "Yes, I believe you."

"I was in love with you. I know what that was like. It was not the same with Pete. He tried to be successful, but some people never make it. No matter what they do or how hard they work, they are failures. It was like that with Pete. I know he wanted Papa's store. I guess

45

he thought if he married me and had the store, he could run it and make out, somehow. But I never had in mind to let him take over the business from me. I know he would have ruined it, even with the best of intentions. He was that kind of a man."

"But you were going to marry him," Durell said.

"Who else is there? A woman must have a man down here, or she dries up and dies in this swamp and heat. I could depend on Pete. He didn't drink or gamble. He was gentle with me." Her face moved, changing. Her mouth shook. "That terrible thing should not have been done to him."

"He had something they wanted. Something you may know about. Jonathan tells me that you went through his stuff and tried to sell it off, the last time, when you thought he was dead. When he was down in Yucatan. If you went through the things he owned, you ought to have some idea of what it might be."

"Oh, God," she said. "That."

"What was it?"

"So Jonathan told you. You must think I'm a greedy bitch."

"I know what you are, Angelina," he said quietly.

"Listen, Pete and I were engaged to be married. His family is gone; there was nobody but me. I tried to run his photo shop for him, at first, but I'm a business woman, not a photographer. Finally, when I gave up hope for him, I decided to close the studio and get rid of everything. What else could I do? Was I supposed to leave all that stuff just to rot?"

"I'm not criticizing you; I just want to know what you might have tried to sell."

She walked away toward the house, then stopped abruptly. Her face was broken. "Maybe I loved Pete in a funny kind of way. Not the way I once loved you, Sam. When I think of those crazy days, I still get a funny feeling inside me. Maybe I'm still in love with you. Would that surprise you?"

"What did you try to sell, Angelina?"

Her eyes searched his face. "It's all gone, isn't it?"

"Angelina, please."

"All right," she said. "I understand you, Sam. I'm sorry. I forgot you're some kind of a cop. That's what your grandpa told me, so I guess you have to ask questions. There wasn't anything valuable. Just a lot of old junk he saved, and his studio equipment. I advertised the cameras and stuff for sale, but there were no buyers. Then I had to go to St. Louis for some supplies for the general store. I do all my own purchasing. I'm not bad at business, you know. You'd be surprised. Anyway, while I was in St. Louis, I saw this ad in the newspapers, asking for war souvenirs, Hitler autographs, that kind of things. I remembered that Pete said he had some papers he liberated, as he said, from some factory in Germany. It was all so long ago. But I remembered it, from going through his things, and I answered the ad. I used a newspaper box because I was just in town for a few days, and I signed my answer A. Greene. That's my business signature. But, anyway, before I even got an answer, I had to come back to Peche Rouge—and there was Pete, home again. He was awful mad at me." She smiled thinly and touched her face with sadly reminiscent fingers. "He slapped me. It was the only time he got rough with me."

"So you never followed up the ad?" Durell asked.

"No."

"Did you look through Pete's things in his bedroom to see if those papers are still there?"

"They're gone, some of them. I looked, because the place was turned inside out when I got here, just before you showed up, Sam. But the war was so long ago! What value could all that junk have today?"

"I wish I knew," Durell said.

"Pete wasted an awful lot of time with those things. That was his trouble. He was a tinkerer. He thought once of going into the photostat business, too, and he spent every night for a month practicing, making copies of all that junk."

Durell halted. They were at the back door of the photo shop. Traffic rumbled on the highway beyond the house, and he felt the vibration of a heavy refrigerator rig rolling north from the shrimp canneries. The ground shook underfoot.

"Pete made photostatic copies?" he asked softly.

"Sure, but—"

"Where are they?"

Angelina shrugged. "I don't know. I can't think. I feel sick now." Her fingers pulled at her mouth and she looked away from him. "In the house someplace, I guess. In the darkroom, maybe."

"Take it easy," he said.

"Why did they do *that* to him?" she whispered again. He had no answer for her.

Chapter Six

S LAGO was drunk. He didn't show it, but Mark knew about it, and he was careful. Slago sprawled on Mark's bed, but Mark made no objection this time. It was the second day since they had picked up Labouisse, since the explosive quarrel over the man's escape. Slago had been drinking steadily, enough to founder an ordinary man. Mark remembered the terror he had felt when they had discovered Labouisse was gone. All that day and night they had been poised for flight, expecting a momentary alarm. But nothing had happened. The man had to be dead. Mark thought that he, too, might have wished for death, after what Slago had done to Labouisse.

Erich had been in a white rage when he learned about Labouisse's escape. "How did it happen? How could you have been so stupid?"

Slago was arrogant, filled with a black excitation. "The punk was out cold. We picked him up and worked him over on a back road out in the swamps, but he'd left his gear at a bar in that fishing town where his boat docked, and we thought we'd better pick it up so nobody would ask questions about it."

Corbin's pale eyes had jumped to Mark. "So you both just left him there?"

Slago shrugged. "It was a pretty buggy place. And Mark was kind of sickish." Slago grinned, his thick-lipped mouth spreading in memory. "I had to work pretty rough on the punk. He was stubborn. And Mark was no damned help at all. So when we came back, he was gone. Crawled away into the water, somehow. But you don't have to worry about him, Erich. He's drowned. Nobody will find him in them swamps."

"If they do, and if he is alive, we are finished."

"It's all right, I tell you. We got what we wanted."

Corbin nodded. "Yes, you did well in that respect."

"Then start making with the chemistry, hey?"

Mark said thinly: "I think we'd better run for it. There's still a chance he'll be found. And there won't be a sheriff anywhere around who could keep the mob back when they find out what Slago had to do to make him talk."

Jessie had turned curiously, then. "What did he do?"

"Slago emasculated him," Mark said flatly.

Jessie's face was expressionless. Mark didn't think she understood. Then she turned and walked out of the room and he watched her through the window as she went into Moon's bar. She didn't come back.

In spite of Mark's caution, Corbin insisted they stand pat and wait where they were. Flight might bring suspicion, too. The proprietor of the camp would describe them to any local cop who nosed around, and Erich's argument sounded cold and logical. Mark's worry had been met by comtempt from Slago. Slago was different; it was as if something had broken down inside him since he had worked on Labouisse. He had been arrogant and loud before; he was infinitely dangerous now, and Mark noted a subtle shift in the relationship between all four of them. His own authority was appreciably weakened. It was true he had moved fast, driving hard back to Peche Rouge, seeing the futility of staying on the coast and trying to track down the escaped man. He had torn through Labouisse's house quickly and efficiently. He had found what they were looking for. Corbin was satisfied with that. Yet Mark felt he had to do something more, to re-establish his authority over them all.

It was growing dark now, and waves of red pulsed through the motel room from the camp's bar. Laughter came from there, and the rough sound of men's voices. A new fishing party had checked in from Arkansas today, three men and two women, all noisy, all guzzling beer. Mark finished shaving and turned to look at Slago sprawled on his bed. Slago had almost emptied the bottle.

"Better cut down on the drinking tonight," Mark told him. "Corbin ought to be ready for the test. It might have some kind of effect Corbin doesn't know about. if you're liquored up."

"Hell, I ain't afraid of no test," Slago said.

"I didn't say you were." There was a germ of an inflection in Slago's thick voice that interested Mark. "It's funny, though, Erich telling *us* to test the stuff while he waits safely outside."

"So?"

"So maybe he doesn't trust his own work," Mark suggested carefully. "Maybe he thinks it might work out differently from the formula."

"Ah, shut up," Slago said. "You chicken, you don't have to do anything."

"Oh, I'll go through with it," Mark said. "It ought to be pretty soon now."

"He'll let us know when," Slago muttered. He kept on drinking.

M ARK stepped outside. It was like breathing steam. Mist hung over the river and made a halo of pink around the neon lights of the bar. Erich's cabin next door was closed. An air conditioner Jessie had gone to New Orleans to buy pulsed quietly in the back window frame. Mark dried his hands on his handkerchief. His fingers felt cool and moist, but he was drenched with sweat. He wished his stomach would settle down, and he wished Jessie would step outside so he could talk to her for just a few moments before the test started. It wasn't that he was afraid, Mark told himself. He had proved his nerve many times, but this was different. A man couldn't help imagining things in a queer setup like this.

Jessie came out of her cabin, as if in answer to his wish. She wore a blue printed silk dress and she had loosened her long yellow hair so it hung smoothly to her shoulders. He watched her walk toward him, remembering how her naked body had looked.

"It's so hot out here," she said quietly.

"Is the air conditioner working all right?"

"It's fine."

"When will Erich be ready?"

"Any minute now. When it gets a bit darker. Did you make a sketch of the bank building?"

Mark nodded. "Do you want to see it?"

"No, that's your business," Jessie said. "It will all be in your hands tomorrow, if everything works out right now."

"Isn't Erich sure it will?"

"He's had to concoct the stuff with makeshift equipment, I guess. He keeps muttering to himself in German. Mark, you be careful with him. He's been after me a lot, since—well, you know."

"Son of a bitch."

She laughed. "Are you jealous?"

"No. Yes. I was thinking he might be sore enough to gimmick the stuff."

"No, he wouldn't do that. It's too important to him." She took him by surprise, then. She moved close to him and put her hands on his chest and her mouth moved against his, in a sudden, fierce passion.

"Do you still want me, darling?" she whispered.

"Sure," he said thickly. "Sure, Jessie."

"Then be patient. After tomorrow, if everything works out, I think our plans will change a little. This is only the beginning, Mark. We have a long way to go, you and I." She stepped back, smiling. "Now give me a cigarette."

They had finished smoking when Erich came out. It was full dark now. Mark went forward to help Erich carry the compressed gas tank around to the back of the Corbin cabin, and they placed it under the window where the air conditioner hummed.

"Is it ready now?" Mark asked.

"It works fine," Erich said shortly. "Get Slago."

Mark returned to his cabin and called to Slago. A car came into the fishing camp and parked at the far end of the row of cabins; the headlights flicked over Jessie's figure standing nearby; then the lights went out and darkness returned. Mark could see Slago sprawled on the bed. The air inside stank of spilled whiskey.

"Slago, come on, get up. We're ready to go."

Slago muttered indistinctly. "Huh?"

"Erich is ready. Let's go."

SLAGO's breath was like a panting animal in the hot, dark cabin. His face was a broad pale wedge turned toward Mark in the doorway; then he turned his face away toward the wall. "I don't feel so good."

"Come on. He's waiting."

"I'll sit this one out," Slago said thickly.

Mark felt a cruel elation lift in him. "You sadistic bastard," he said softly. "You're the one who's chicken. You're afraid."

"Watch your mouth, buddy boy."

51

"Then get up. Everything is ready."

"I guess I drank too much."

"Get up," Mark said thinly.

He walked into the cabin to his suitcase near the dresser and took out his gun. Dim neon light washed redly through the open doorway and showed him the man on the bed. He pointed the gun at Slago. "Get up, you son of a bitch."

Slago lifted himself on his elbows and stared. Mark could smell the acid of his sweat. He wasn't worried about Slago any more. It didn't matter what the man had done to those others. They had been helpless. Slago was good under those conditions. He wasn't so tough right now.

"You're going through with it, Slago," Mark said. "We're both walking into that cabin and we'll stay there until it's all over, understand?"

"Hell, what've we got to test it for, if Erich is so good?"

"It's got to be tested. Let's go."

"Buddy boy, put away that gun. You won't plug me here."

"Try me," Mark said.

The juke box in the bar across the way began to thump out a rock-and-roll tune. Slago rubbed his jaw with his big hand and coughed and stood up, hitching up his pants.

"You first," Mark said.

They stood in the dark behind Corbin's cabin, while Erich fiddled with the control valves on the small steel tank Jessie had picked up in New Orleans. If Erich was aware of Slago's fear, he paid no attention. But Jessie knew.

"Are you all right, Mark?"

"Fine," he said quickly.

"You, Slago?"

"I ain't gonna do it," Slago muttered.

"Yes, you are," Mark said. "Either you do it, or you can start walking away and don't come back."

"Who stops me from comin' back?"

"I do," Mark said.

Slago licked his lips and shrugged. Mark pushed him ahead into Corbin's cabin and closed the door behind them. The air in here felt icy after the dense humidity outside. Jessie's perfume clung lightly in the air. The air conditioner hummed in the back window. Mark turned the bolt in the door and walked around Slago, who stood frozen in the dim light of the bed lamp. Corbin rapped on the window.

"All right," Mark said to Slago. "This is it. Sit down and relax."

Slago made a thin sound in his throat and suddenly whirled, clawing at the door to escape. Mark jumped after him and brought the butt of his gun hard on the cropped salt-and-pepper skull. Slago half turned, his mouth opened, his eyes glazing. He fell to his knees, making queer sounds. Blood ran down from the cut in his scalp.

Mark looked down at him and laughed.

He deliberately drew several deep, long breaths. He didn't smell anything, didn't feel anything.

He heard a faint hissing over the hum of the air conditioner and then he felt just a faint giddiness before his legs buckled as if every muscle had been cut and he went sliding into sudden darkness. He fell over Slago and felt the man swing at him feebly and he kept on laughing until the darkness washed over him in a great, drowning wave. Only then did he feel a sudden, despairing panic.

Chapter Seven

WE'RE golden," Slago said triumphantly, grinning broadly. "Erich, you're a genius."

"It was not too difficult."

"I'm not even sore at you, Mark."

"Thanks for nothing," Mark said.

Erich smiled. "You both feel all right? No ill effects?"

"It was as smooth as whipped cream," Mark said.

"It would have been better if Slago had not fallen and hurt his head. It leaves a question about the potency of the amount of gas I allowed to be pulled into the room."

Slago said quickly: "So I stumbled and fell. I was on my way to dreamland, anyway." He looked at Mark. "Right?"

"You didn't stumble. I slugged you, because you were ready to chicken out," Mark said. "Now shut up."

It was twenty minutes later. They were gathered in Corbin's cabin. The air conditioner again hummed innocuously, and the air was cool and refreshing. Mark felt infinitely better about everything. His stomach was quiet now. He took the sketches he had made of the Peche Rouge National Bank and spread them on the bed. His hand brushed Jessie's hip, but she did not move, and Erich said nothing.

"We take the bank tomorrow," Mark said. "Every window is sealed tight, and the doors are kept closed, too. They open at nine, as usual. Slago and I go in at nine-thirty. Erich, you looked at the air vents today. Can you reach them easily?"

Corbin nodded and poked his rimless glasses up on his sharp nose. "In the alley. I can reach the ducts."

"The cylinder isn't too heavy?"

"I can do my part."

"What about the nose guards?"

"They are ready. How do you think I came in here to wake you up?" He held out two small rolls of saturated cotton wadding that he had withdrawn from his nostrils earlier. "The gas will not affect either of you, so long as you remember to breathe through these, in your nose. When the people in the bank go down, you just help yourselves. Take all the money you want. You will have more than ten minutes, and nobody will remember you."

Slago slapped his thick leg. "We're golden, I tell you. Think of it, buddy boy. Every goddam bank in the country has air conditioning these days, all summer long, especially down around here. There ain't a building we can't walk into, once Erich starts spraying his holy perfume into the ducts."

Jessie spoke quietly. "But it will be for peanuts. A few thousands here and there. But the whole country will soon enough be alarmed."

Slago was still excited by his thoughts. "So we work fast, baby. We knock over one or two a day."

"For how long?" she asked.

Slago blinked his small eyes. "This is a new tune you're singin' all of a sudden, sweetheart. What's eating you? We talked all this out before. By the time the word gets around the country that no air conditioned bank is safe, we'll have it made, baby."

"Don't call me baby," Jessie said.

"What's eating you?" Slago asked again.

"We'll try it tomorrow. Just once, to really test it." She spoke with a quiet authority that Mark did not miss. He glanced at Erich, but the chemist was silent, bent over the equipment he had packed into one of the closets. Jessie went on: "I have other ideas on how we can use Erich's gas. If we waste it on small-town banks, we might take perhaps a hundred thousand, maybe even mroe. But that's still peanuts. Once the alarm gets out, every bank in the country will remodel their setup so we can't get at the ducts. They'll work fast, believe me. And they'll know about us. The thing we must do is to strike once, at something very big. One big strike, do you understand?"

"Where?" Mark asked quietly.

Slago sneered. "Fort Knox, maybe?"

"Something better than Fort Knox," Jessie said. Her manner was still quietly assured as she stood up. "We'll discuss it tomorrow, when we're on our way out of here."

Slago was angry. "Who's givin' orders now?"

"I am," Jessie said.

THE Peche Rouge National Bank faced the courthouse on the square. It was open from nine to three daily, and most its customers were the townspeople, but it also served the fishing and canning industry, as well as some of the offshore oil riggers who made Bayou Peche Rouge a financial base of operations.

Wednesday was usually slow, the day before the cannery payroll, and sometimes an hour would go by while Miss Bunting, the teller, and Amos Roy Freeling, the manager, sat idly in the cool comfort of the air-conditioned interior, with no one coming into the building at all. On this Wednesday morning, at 9:05, a tourist had come in to cash two hundred dollars' worth of travelers checks, and then nothing happened for the next twenty minutes.

Miss Bunting was happy with her job. She felt cool and fresh in her now cotton dress, unlike the red-faced perspiring people who occasionally crossed her vision beyond the big plate window that faced the courthouse square. It was hot out there, and it would get hotter as the day went on. But in here, thanks to the system Mr. Amos had had installed last year, it was cool and dry and comfortable. At first, some of the tradespeople would step in to gossip, just to hang around and cool off. But Mr. Roy was uneasy about that and he had quickly put a stop to the practice. Now people came in on business, or not at all.

Miss Bunting noticed the tall man with the curly blonde hair the moment he paused outside. The square was somnolent in the morning sunshine. She noticed Mark Fleming only because he was a stranger. She would have been surprised at how much Mark knew about her.

He came in and went immediately to the counters where blank checks and deposit slips were available to the bank's customers. Now and then he put a handkerchief to his nose. The cotton wads that Corbin had provided for his nostrils were uncomfortable, and the chemical solution that acted as a neutralizing agent made his eyes smart. He looked like a man with hay fever, Miss Bunting thought. He busied himself with a deposit slip, but his thoughts were intent on what was happening in the street behind the bank.

He had done his part of the job. He knew the doors could be locked with a simple hand latch on the inside. Only three steps, and he could seal the bank against interruption. The gray-haired woman in the teller's cage was watching him, but he wasn't worried about her. The manager, in his glass-partitioned cubicle, was running an adding machine. The vault stood open in the rear. There was a guard, an old man in a shabby gray uniform, in a chair in the room beside the vault. There was a back door to the bank, but it was sealed and barred and never used.

The street behind the building was residential, with gray two-family frame houses, a few trees, picket fences, and lawns. At the same moment Mark had entered the bank, Slago and Erich walked down the street carrying the tank and a box of tools. They wore jumpers that made them look like repairmen. A teen-aged kid fixing a bicycle in one of the front yards scarcely glanced at them. Nobody else was interested enough to step out into the hot sun and watch.

At 9:35 Slago unfolded a small canvas hood and stepped up on a small box to enclose the vanes of the air-conditioner inlet duct set into the rear wall of the bank building. The burglar alarm was fixed higher to the wall, and he grinned at it. No need to worry about cops piling in on their heels. Nobody would give the alarm until it was long over, which was the beautiful part of this deal. Corbin handed up the pressure tank. The boy fixing his bike put down his wrench and sat down on the lawn to watch Slago now. Slago opened the valve on the tank cylinder and directed the jet nozzle under the canvas hood, into the air-conditioning vent. The hissing noise sounded loud in the hot, sunny stillness.

The boy on the lawn got up and walked diagonally across the street to get a better look at what was going on.

It was 9:40.

Jessie entered the bank through the front door. The Cadillac was parked in a slot directly in front of the building. She looked cool in a full cotton skirt and blouse, with a pink ribbon in her yellow hair. She paused just inside the door, as if to adjust her eyes to the interior shadows, and Mark smiled and went to her. With her body shielding the lock on the door from Miss Bunting's gaze, Mark was able to turn the latch without observation.

The bank was now sealed.

Unless a customer arrived in the next few minutes and created a disturbance trying to get in, there would be no trouble at all.

MARK moved toward Miss Bunting's cage. He was conscious of the discomfort of the nasal wads and the distortion of his voice when he spoke.

"I would like to open a checking account, please," he said, and smiled. "Perhaps you had better take me to Mr. Freeling. It will not be a business account, however. Just personal. I'm here only for a short time."

"I see. Are you visiting Peche Rouge for business purposes, though?"

"You might call it that," Mark said.

He watched her pink face closely. Tension was building in him. The gas ought to be going in by now. It ought to start its sudden work at any moment. But there was no change in Miss Bunting's brisk movements as she left her booth and walked around to open the gate that led to Mr. Freeling's cubicle. Suppose Erich's gas didn't work this time? Or suppose the nasal wads that

57

should keep him conscious for six or seven minutes failed to do the job? He heard the front door rattle suddenly. A bulky man with gray hair and fisherman's clothes stood there, a bank book in his thick hand. Jessie was moving toward the door to wave him off.

"This way, please," Miss Bunting said.

She looked curiously at the door where the customer stood rattling the knob. "Why doesn't he come in?" she said impatiently. Then she looked at Mr. Freeling, behind his desk. "Mr. Amos—is anything the matter?"

The pudgy bank manager held his head in his hands. Miss Bunting looked alarmed. She sat down suddenly and her hand went to her throat. "Oh, dear, I—"

Her face went white. She began to tip to one side and Mark put his hand on her shoulder and straightened her out on the chair. Her frail body felt boneless.

He spoke to Freeling. "Hey, you son of a bitch."

The bank manager didn't move. Elation shot through Mark. He looked toward the front door. Jessie had her back to the street, but the fisherman was still outside, looking confused.

"Where is the guard?" Jessie called. "Make sure of him, Mark."

"Get that man away from there!" he said harshly.

"I can't. And don't talk any more. You'll breathe—Mark!"

It was too late. He had forgotten Corbin's repeated warning and had inhaled through his mouth. A wave of dizziness swept him, and he felt his legs turn rubbery. A strange curiosity touched him when he found himself on his knees beside Freeling's desk. He saw Jessie through a vast, darkening distance.

"Mark?"

Her voice echoed back and forth in the black caverns of his mind. He was aware of dismay, anger, sudden panic; but he didn't open his mouth again to gasp or yell. He inhaled deeply through his nostrils, through the nose wads stuffed in the breathing passages. Weakness kept him down. He told himself to get up, but he couldn't. Precious time was slipping away, sliding away like quicksand. Jesus, he thought, I've wrecked it now! He forced his panic down and drew another deep, careful breath through his nose. His hand came up and he looked at it and he hauled himself up by pulling at the edge of Freeling's desk. He looked curiously at the bank manager

58

and Miss Bunting. They seemed like wax images, paralyzed, not moving. How much time was left? Five minutes? Four? There was only a small quantity of the gas in Erich's portable pressure tank.

What was Jessie doing? He heard her sharp footsteps on the marble floor, moving through the teller's gate. She was scooping up loose cash from Miss Bunting's cage, cramming it into the big straw handbag she carried. Mark forced himself to move down the short hallway to the vault. The old bank guard had fallen from his chair and lay shriveled on the floor. The vault was open. There was a pile of currency in an open box. The keys, he thought. Where are the keys? He started to hunt aimlessly, then scooped up the visible cash and went back to Jessie and dropped it into her handbag. Her eyes were scornful. Only two or three minutes were left.

The fisherman had gone away from the front door.

IT SEEMED endless, but finally it was done. All the money in sight had been shoved into Jessie's handbag. They would have to be content with it. Mark waved to the door and Jessie spoke, exhaling as she formed the words.

"Are you all right now?"

He nodded. A groan came from Mr. Freeling, sprawled at his desk. He would be revived in a moment. Miss Bunting was stirring, too.

"Let's get out of here."

Mark turned the thumb latch on the door and they stepped out into the hot blast of sunshine that baked the courthouse square. Jessie went straight to the parked Cadillac with the handbag. There was no alarm. Nothing had disturbed the tranquility of the town. Miss Bunting and Mr. Freeling, thanks to the peculiar actions of Erich's gas, would scarcely remember them. Certainly not enough to give the police an adequate description. Then Mark saw the gray-haired, burly fisherman who had been at the bank door. He was across the square, talking to a dark-haired girl who had come out of the general store. Both the fisherman and the girl were staring at him. The fisherman's arms moved in quick, excited gestures, and then the girl put a hand on his shoulder, as if to restrain him.

"Hurry," Jessie said thinly. Mark nodded and started to pull the irritating wads from his nostrils, and she said: "Don't throw them away here. Get in."

"That local spotted us. Over there, with that girl."

"Never mind. There isn't time. Let's go."

He got into the car with her and she backed easily out of the slot and drove around a corner of the square. A few cars moved slowly in traffic across the way, and some pedestrians walked on the diagonal walks under the live oaks in the square. Everything was quiet.

"How much do you think we got?" Mark asked.

"Not enough. You almost went under, didn't you?"

"I'm sorry. I forgot."

"Don't apologize," Jessie said coldly. "I shouldn't have spoken to you in there. I almost forgot about it, myself."

They turned the corner. Slago and Erich were waiting for them with the equipment. The canvas hood had been removed from the air-conditioning vent in the back wall of the bank building. Slago heaved the pressure tank into the back seat.

A boy in blue jeans lay sprawled in the shadows by the rear door of the bank.

"What happened?" Mark asked.

"A nosey kid," Slago rumbled. "I put him out."

"Did he get a good look at you?"

Erich said nervously: "He saw us, but I am sure he will be afraid to talk, after Slago."

"I don't like it," Mark said. "We were spotted by a couple on the other side of the building, too."

Jessie drove the Cad out of the side street. Mark looked back at the courthouse square. The fisherman and the dark-haired girl were walking rapidly toward a car parked in front of the general store.

They were halfway out of town before Miss Bunting came to the front door and began her confused screaming.

Chapter Eight

D URELL drove his rented car into the parking lot in downtown New Orleans and left it there. The Galleon Bar was off St. Charles, a businessman's luncheon place decorated with fake beams and yellow-glass ship's lanterns and a half-hearted attempt to instill a pirate atmosphere into the fixtures. Big wooden fans slowly stirred the air around the booths beyond the bar.

Durell walked slowly back toward the booths, which were all occupied, mostly by men. One booth had four women in it. They looked like tourists.

It was noon of the third day since he had found Pierre Labouisse in the pirogue, and he felt as if he had stood still while time raced by and he accomplished nothing.

Turning, he walked back to the bar and found a stool. He ordered bourbon from the fat bartender and looked at a very bad oil painting above the racked tiers of bottles on their mirrored shelves. A young man who looked as if he wasn't many years out of college came in and took the stool next to him and looked at Durell's drink and ordered bourbon, too.

Then they looked at each other in the mirror.

"Like our weather, Sam?"

"I was born to it," Durell said.

"This place all right?"

"Good enough," Durell said.

"Why not my office?"

"You have secretaries. Other agents, in and out."

"So? Is it that restricted?"

"Top secret."

"I'm flattered."

"Then get with it," Durell said. "What did you pick up?"

The young man's name was Kevin MacCreedy. He was a field agent out of the New Orleans district office of the Federal Bureau of Investigation, but he was not in charge of the office. His name had been given to Durell by Daniel Kincaid in Washington. MacCreedy wore a fine Panama straw, a suit of pale cream, and mesh shoes. He had slick blond hair and a cheerful face and his eyes were a dark gray. He looked like a young lawyer or a young businessman or something equally innocuous. Last year he had walked unarmed up a flight of tenement steps in the French Quarter and with a shattered left shoulder he had taken Redleg Greer, third on the wanted list.

"You want a report here?" MacCreedy asked.

The fat bartender was at the other end of the bar. "Yes."

"We've got Labouisse on ice. Literally. Officially, he's

61

still listed as a missing person, and the local sheriff is beating the bayous for him. There'll be some friction when it comes out we've been holding the body. How long do we sit on it?"

"Not much longer," Durell said.

"Somebody did a wicked job on him."

"Did you check Joe Tibault's boat and crew?"

"Personally. We know Fleming met Labouisse, picked him up, and they drove away together. Old war buddies, hey? We know it was Fleming from the description you gave us. Tibault has good eyes, too."

"How many men have you got looking for Fleming now?"

"Not enough. An even half-dozen, including me. You want more, Sam, you'll have to ask Washington. Who are you working with now, anyway?"

Durell said: "Do you have to know?"

"Well, you swing a lot of weight, that's all."

"You haven't uncovered any rocks where Fleming and his crowd might be hiding?"

"We're working the highways, motels, tourist homes —that sort of thing. The delta is a big territory. Happy vacation paradise for one and all. So is New Orleans. They could be in town. They could in Mobile. They could be on the moon."

"They're here," Durell said.

"Maybe the locals could help."

"No local cops on this," Durell said. "Just keep looking. What about the photostats I gave you?"

"We got a lab report back on it from Washington." MacCreedy looked at the bartender, who was wiping the bar nearby, and ordered another bourbon. When the fat man slid his glass toward him, MacCreedy waited until he went farther away. "It's part of a chemical formula for an anesthetic gas, they think. Sort of a nerve gas, an ether derivative. Nothing sensational. No real military application, anyway."

"Then why do they want it so badly?"

"Who?"

"The lad who did the art work with the knife. And his friends."

MacCreedy drank his bourbon. "Search me. Washington isn't excited. At least, my office isn't. They're not sure, mind you, because the whole formula isn't there. It will take some lab research to work it out. Maybe we'll hear more about it by tomorrow." MacCreedy paused. "Meanwhile, what do I do with the body on ice?"

"Can you hold it for another twenty-four hours?"

"Sure. But the sheriff will be sore as hell for holding out a murder on him. And the newspapers will jump on the mutilation angle."

"See that they don't get it. It's important. The people I'm after have to keep thinking Labouisse died in the swamp and hasn't been found."

MacCreedy shook his head. "I don't understand, but you're the boss, Sam. Washington says to give you anything you ask for."

"I'll have another bourbon," Durell said.

FOR two days he had worked with MacCreedy and come up with nothing, no sign of Erich Corbin or his wife, or Mark Fleming and Slago. He was sure Slago was with the group now. Washington had not been able to turn up a trace of the man anywhere in the country, and a memo from Wittington via MacCreedy had advised him that a connection had been made between Fleming and Slago in New York, over three months ago, prior to Slago's subsequent disappearance. Slago had been in a trucking racket, which made him all of a piece with Fleming's background. Thinking about this accomplished little for Durell. He still had no idea where to find them, nor could he guess what they would do next.

He left the FBI man a few minutes later. The noonday heat on the street was intense. He wondered if he ought to return to Washington, and then he walked down to the corner and a headline caught his eye and he stopped.

The Bayou Peche Rouge National Bank had been robbed.

Mysterious circumstances were hinted. Nobody had seen the robbers. A strange gas apparently had been introduced into the ducts of the air-conditioning system, stunning the occupants for some ten minutes while the robbers helped themselves to the ready cash. Apparently the robbers had used an antidote that rendered them immune to the gas.

Over seventeen thousand dollars had been taken.

DURELL drove south from the city to Peche Rouge. It was one o'clock when he parked on the landing beside his grandfather's steamboat. The hulk looked

63

calm and placid in the sunlight that laved the dark bayou. As he got out, his elbow touched the horn ring of the Chevy, and the sharp blast momentarily disrupted the misty beauty of the scene. Herons and pelicans flapped away into the dark gloom of the cypress groves on the opposite shore. Jonathan came out on deck and called to him.

"You heard about the robbery, Samuel?"

"I heard. I'm looking for Angelina. Have you seen her?"

The white-haired old man stood erect and alert. "You look upset, Samuel. Has the bank business anything to do with your business?"

"I think so. Have you seen Angelina?"

"Them people walked in right after nine this morning. Nobody in the bank but old Miss Bunting and Amos Freeling. Kind of mixed up about the number of customers inside at the time. Hear tell they all just went to sleep on their feet for ten, fifteen minutes while the bandits helped themselves." He paused. "Yes, Angelina was here, Samuel. She was looking for you, about an hour ago. She said she had something important to tell you, but she wouldn't say what it was when I told her you were in New Orleans. I don't think you ought to see her, though."

Durell looked at his grandfather. They were both of the same height. "Why not, Grandpa?"

"She's still in love with you, that's why not."

"She was going to marry Pete Labouisse." He knew at once he had made a slip, speaking about Pete in the past tense. The old man was very alert. "Maybe she loves him still, for all I know."

"She won't marry Pete," Jonathan said. "You know that, eh? She told you she changed her mind?"

"Well—" Durell said.

"I didn't teach you as well as I thought, Samuel. You don't play poker the way you should."

"I never could win from you, anyway, Grandpa."

"What happened to Pete?"

"Nothing you have to know. Where can I find Angelina?"

"She went off to meet Joe Tibault. How come Joe is back from shrimping and Pete ain't around?"

"Where is Joe?"

"When you don't answer a question, Samuel, it means

64

you got an answer you don't want me to have. All right, I won't pry. And you're right, I'm still better at poker than you are, son. Angelina will give you trouble—maybe the kind of trouble you like, a woman like that—but I keep thinkin' of Deirdre Padgett."

"She's in Europe."

"That's no excuse, Samuel."

Durell was irritated for a moment, then he smiled. "You're right, it's no excuse. Where can I find Joe and Angelina?"

"At Mama Juliette's."

"Thanks, Grandpa."

Mama Juliette's was a bar near the shrimp docks in Peche Rouge. It had a tin roof and one of the biggest live oaks in the parish growing right in front of the main entrance so customers had to walk around it in order to get inside. It was air conditioned, Durell noted. He wondered how long it would take for the alarm to spread throughout the country.

Mama Juliette was old and fat, with white hair cut in a masculine style. She was Creole, and most of the time she insisted on speaking French, especially to customers she did not like. She knew Durell very well, and when he stepped into the cool, beery interior, she crooked a fat finger at him and he followed to a table in back of the bar.

"Angelina left a message for you, Sam."

"How long ago?"

"Twenty minutes, maybe. You heard about the bank robbery?" Mama Juliette laughed. "They got over thirty thousand, I hear."

Durell did not correct her. "Where did Angelina go? Did she say what she wanted to see me about?"

"Hey, boy, you want her bad? Don't forget she's spoken for."

"Does she really get around much, Mama?"

Mama Juliette shook her head. "She's a good girl. I shouldn't talk that way about her. It's just the way she looks, and the way the men look at the way she looks. right? I used to be like that, once. Hard to believe, hey?"

"Was she with Joe Tibault?"

"Sure. They said for you to go to Moon's Fishing Camp and walk light. They'll meet you on the road. What's it all about, Sam?"

"It's an easy way to pull teeth," Durell said.

"What?"

"I was thinking of something else. Thanks, Mama."

"There was a cop around here, couple days ago. He didn't say he was a cop, but he was from the city, and he was asking about Pete and Angelina. It was kind of funny. I mean, funny-strange. I didn't tell him anything. Why should I tell a city man anything about our people?"

"That's right, Mama," he said.

It explained why MacCreedy's men had made no progress.

MOON'S camp was a short drive to the west, along a secondary road that bordered a bayou canal. Durell drove slowly along the graveled road. He wondered why Angelina wanted to see him so urgently, and why she hadn't waited for him either at the steamboat or at Mama Juliette's. And why she was with Joe Tibault.

He didn't see her car when he drove past the camp, and he didn't stop there. He went around a narrow bend in the road and then he saw her yellow convertible parked in the brush, partly screened by Spanish moss hanging from the gnarled limbs that spanned across the sky overhead. He stopped alongside and got out. Nobody was in sight. Through the foliage he saw the canal, and a man rowing by in a skiff, a fishing rod hanging over the transom. He didn't know the man, who looked like a tourist, and Durell walked back toward the camp.

The main cabin, containing the bar, was built of rude cypress logs, with red neon signs advertising beer below another sign that simply read: *Moon's*. About half the cabins were occupied, to judge by the number of parked cars, and he noted the Cadillac with the California plates at once, but he didn't look that way again. At this hour, in the full smother of the afternoon heat, no one was around.

There were two men in the bar, talking in Northern accents, and Jake Moon himself. Durell knew Moon, but Moon did not remember him. The last time Durell had seen the camp proprietor, he had been no more than twelve or thirteen. He did not see Angelina or Joe Tibault.

He sat down and ordered beer. The normal sounds of the fishing camp came to him. Nothing more. The beer was not as cold as it could have been. Through the fly-speckled window, seen through the tubing of the neon signs, he watched the cabin where the California Cad was parked. The shades were down, and there were no signs of life. He watched it, anyway.

There was no doubt in his mind that the robbery of the bank was the work of Corbin and Fleming. Durell wasn't worried about the stolen money. It was the method of stealing it that interested him. And the further plans that Corbin might have. He tried to project his mind along the lines that Erich Corbin might be thinking, but he could see nothing except a further series of robberies based on this method, a quick wave of assaults that might temporarily disrupt small-town banks with certain types of air-conditioning systems. But it would only be temporary. And Corbin was no fool. From his past record, his moves indicated more to come. Something far more important. He tried to think what it could be, but he couldn't come up with anything.

He felt concerned about Angelina. Where was she? Why had she come here with Joe Tibault?

"Sam?"

He heard her call. Her voice sounded thin and unnatural. He turned his head and saw her beyond the screen door of the bar, standing in the harsh sunlight of the parking area. He got up and went outside to her. She touched his arm briefly and started walking toward the floats along the Peche Rouge canal, where skiffs and pirogues and a few outboards were moored. The sun made glowing highlights on her sleek black hair. Her face was very pale. She wore a full skirt this time, and a man's white shirt, open at the throat.

"What's up?" he asked. "What are you doing here?"

"Joe saw those men," she said tensely. Her breathing was ragged, as if she had been running. He saw by her eyes that she was afraid of something. "The two who met Pete down along the shore and took him away."

"Take it slowly," he told her.

"They were in town this morning, just before the bank robbery. The good-looking one and the hoodlum. He saw them drive away after the robbery, too. He knows they were in the bank when it happened. But Joe didn't know what was happening, you see? I mean, he didn't know they were robbing the bank. He was watching them, and everything was quiet, and he didn't dare go call the

67

sheriff or anybody; he wanted to keep them in sight. And then they came out and he came over to my store and I got my car and we followed them. First to Mama Juliette's. I took a chance and came to your grandfather's, but you weren't there. I got back in time, though. Then they came here. Don't look at that car now, Sam. Did you see it?"

"Yes," Durell said. "Where is Joe?"

"They've got him," Angelina said.

D URELL halted on one of the docks. A boat shed screened them from the cabins. "Are you listening?" Angelina asked. "Joe is sure those are the men who picked up Pete. Sam, please. What are we going to do?"

"Where did they take Joe?"

"Into one of the cabins. The ugly one saw us on the road, just after we parked. He had a gun. I ran away, but Joe stayed to give me a chance to escape."

"Have you heard anything from inside the cabin?"

"No, not a sound. What are they doing to him?"

"Have you called anyone? The police?"

"Not yet."

Durell thought of MacCreedy, in New Orleans. There was a telephone in Jake Moon's bar. It would take too long, he thought. He thought of the man with the knife, wondering if it was Slago. He knew there was no time to get help. Then he turned to Angelina again. She was biting her lip. He gave her MacCreedy's number.

"Go into the bar the back way," he told her. "Don't take a chance showing on that parking lot again. Call this number, ask for a Mr. MacCreedy. Tell him where we are. Tell him to put a cork in it."

"Put a cork—"

"He'll understand. Go ahead, now."

She looked dubious. "What are you going to do?"

"I'll be around."

She seemed afraid to leave him. He pushed her gently up the slope toward Moon's bar. When she started walking, Durell turned and circled the boat shed and walked up through the tall weeds toward the far end of the row of cabins. The right thing to do, he told himself, was to wait for MacCreedy. Never mind about Joe Tibault. But he didn't like the silence in that cabin. Joe could be dead by now. But maybe he wasn't. If he waited, every minute that went by increased the chances that Joe would join the other victims. Durell had known the shrimp fisherman all his life. He didn't like to think of what might be happening to him right now. And what might happen if he sat tight and waited for MacCreedy to gather his men and post roadblocks around the area. He couldn't wait for that. It would take twenty minutes, maybe half an hour, for the net to start closing. Too long. He couldn't let Joe stay in that cabin for that length of time.

He walked faster. His hand was on the gun in his pocket.

There was a new air conditioner in the back window of the cabin where the Cadillac was parked, and this interested him, because none of the other cabins were so equipped; he was sure Moon hadn't provided it. He began to feel a familiar excitement that came to him when his quarry was near. Durell had every instinct of the professional hunter. All his senses were honed razor-sharp. He paused in the angular shadow behind the cabin next to the one where the Cadillac was parked. A bird he didn't recognize sang in a treetop nearby. Somebody revved up an outboard motor downstream. A faint wind made a rustling sound in the brush, and when it touched him, it felt like the dank breath of a fevered animal.

There were footsteps in the cabin where he paused. A man's voice rumbled something, and something else thudded heavily to the floor inside. The shades were drawn in the window, and he could not look in. He wondered if Angelina had reached the bar.

All at once a heavy, dead silence settled over the place. Then he heard her scream, and everything came apart.

HE SAW her an instant later, bursting through the front entrance of Moon's bar. She was running, her skirt billowing, hampering her. A man came after her at a dead run. Short and squat, with cropped salt-and-pepper hair, with the musculature of a bull. He moved extraordinarily fast, grabbed at her shoulder, and twisted hard. Angelina fell in the dust of the parking area. She was still screaming. A knife flashed in the man's hand, and Durell's gun cracked almost of its own volition. He had aimed for the man's wrist, and he hit the knife instead. It shattered, spinning away in broken pieces into

69

the dust. The man looked up, his mouth open in surprise. Angelina tried to scramble away, but the man grabbed her and hauled her roughly to her feet, one thick arm around her waist, holding her as a shield.

Durell stepped out between the cabins.

"Let her loose, Slago!"

The man cursed in a gravelly voice. Jake Moon came to the door of his bar and hastily retreated again. Slago began pushing Angelina ahead of him across the open area, advancing toward the Cadillac. Durell took a step and then there was movement behind him and he glimpsed a man behind him, arm upraised, a gun reversed in his hand. He took the blow on his shoulder as he turned, and felt the pain jolt down into his gun hand. He couldn't hold the gun. It fell into the dust and he went down to one knee, still turning, and grabbed for a hold on the man who had surprised him.

It was Mark Fleming. Durell got his arm up to partially block a second blow. The thought flickered through his mind that he had been too intent on Slago and Angelina, and he knew the penalty of carelessness. He tried to get up, but Fleming kicked him expertly, his heel cracking on Durell's chest. Durell went over backward, got to his hands and knees, and drove for the gun he had dropped. Fleming kicked it away.

"Copper?" Fleming breathed.

His gun was coming up, not reversed now. Then a screen door slammed, and from the corner of his eye Durell saw Erich Corbin and a blonde girl come out quickly, moving toward the Cadillac. Slago had Angelina's arm twisted up behind her back, running her toward the car, too. They were going to get away.

There was no sign of Joe Tibault.

"Get up, mister," Fleming said. His voice, in his boyish face, seemed harsh. His gun was a Colt .38. "Get up, quick."

Durell stood. His mind raced, assessing the situation. Corbin shouted to Slago; the blonde girl was already in the car. They were pulling out. He suddenly knew they would take Angelina with them as a hostage, if they could. Corbin was throwing a suitcase into the car. Angelina's safety took precedence over other factors at the moment. In other circumstances he might have sacrificed her, as he had been trained and conditioned to do. But not now; the issue was not that desperate.

He went for Fleming's gun. Fleming was careful, but not careful enough, and Durell almost made it.

He chopped the gun from Fleming's fingers. His foot caught Fleming's knee and the man screamed and spun about and went down. At the same moment, Angelina broke loose and ran, twisting out of Slago's reach. She was heading back to the bar, where the other customers stood frozen in fear. Corbin yelled to Slago to forget the girl and the chunky man hesitated, then ran toward the Cadillac. Fleming got to his feet. Durell hit him across the bridge of his nose, hit him again in the stomach, and Fleming reeled back, arms flailing, and smashed into the car. Durell was almost there when the blonde jumped out. He didn't see what she had in her hand. There was no time. For an instant, he allowed his glance to be diverted toward Angelina, running for the bar. She was almost there.

Something struck the side of his head. At the same time, the Cadillac started with a lurch, backing out between the cabins. The rear tires spun savagely and spit gravel over him in a stinging spray. He jumped aside, his head still ringing from whatever the girl had hit him with. She had slipped between the cabins and as Durell jumped, he felt the sleek fender of the car rip at his leg. It felt as if something had grabbed him and flung him bodily against the cabin wall. The scene reeled away into a misty darkness. He was on his hands and knees in the dust, shaking his head, dimly aware that the Cadillac had stopped, that the girl and Slago were helping Fleming into the back seat.

Durell tried to get up. His gun, and Fleming's, still glittered in the gravel, twenty feet away. He heard the roar of the car's motor and felt gritty dust between his teeth, and then the roaring car swung toward the road.

Chapter Nine

DURELL got slowly to his feet. He felt bruised and shaken, but this did not trouble him as much as the fact that he had allowed his quarry to escape. A shouted question came from the bar. Jake Moon had stepped cautiously out into the dust left by the Cadillac's wild flight, Angelina behind him. She came running to him. "Are you all right, Sam?"

"Not exactly." He picked up his gun and then the Colt he had knocked out of Mark Fleming's hand. He pocketed them both. He smiled thinly. "My pride is bruised. Did you call MacCreedy before Slago got to you?"

She shook her head. "I didn't have a chance. He knew that Joe and I had followed him from town. He sneaked up on me in the bar. He—he touched me—like an animal —" Her dark eyes were very wide, remembering. "What about Joe? Have you seen him?"

"I'll look." He turned her back toward the bar. "Go ahead, call MacCreedy. And have Moon call the local sheriff. We'll need to close off the roads."

"All right."

He watched her turn back toward the excited men in the bar entrance, and then he swung about and walked into Corbin's cabin.

The air conditioner still hummed quietly in the back window. Clothing was scattered on the beds, and two suitcases had been left behind, partially packed, abandoned in their sudden flight. Durell didn't touch anything. He rolled up the front window shades and heard a muffled sound from the bathroom, and went there and found Joe Tibault. The fisherman was bound and gagged, and he had bitten the inside of his mouth in his effort to scream. He had needed to scream, Durell thought bitterly. One arm had been dislocated, and there were knife wounds on his hands. Two fingers had been sliced off. He had been questioned expertly, without mercy. Slago obviously had wanted to know more about Joe Tibault and why Joe and Angelina had followed them back to the fishing camp. The gag had kept the shrimp fisherman from making noise during his moments of horror.

"It's all right, Joe." Durell knelt beside the chunky, gray-haired fisherman and untied the gag. A gush of blood ran over the man's lip and down his chin. He coughed weakly, his hand on Durell's arm. "Can you hear me? You'll be all right now."

"Crazy . . ." Tibault whispered. "The one with the knife. Laughing, saying he was going to carve me up . . . butchering me . . ." He looked at his bloody hand, where the two fingers were missing. Under his olive

72

tan, his face was pale and moistly shining. His mouth worked for a moment and he coughed again, and spit out more blood. "Angelina?"

"She's phoning the cops. Stay here, Joe. I'll get a doctor."

"Never mind the doctor. Get them."

"We'll do our best, Joe."

THREE hours later Durell parked in the courthouse square of Bayou Peche Rouge and walked into the little park. He chose a bench under a live oak facing the courthouse, lit a cigarette, and waited for MacCreedy to come out of the bank nearby. The town, the square, the bench itself was as familiar to him as the palm of his hand. He remembered a night many years ago when he had sat on this bench with Angelina. He remembered the warm taste of her young lips, the amazing softness of her mouth as she kissed him. Babes in the wood, he thought. It was all over and done with. They were grown up now. Her father, who had resented him, had loomed in those days as an ogre, a spying, evil-tempered old man who had viewed him with suspicion—justifiably, Durell thought, grinning—and had cursed his daughter as a loose woman. The old man was dead now. It was all dead.

MacCreedy came out of the bank and walked into the park. It was after five in the afternoon. Durell had decided not to appear publicly here as an arm of the law. It was MacCreedy's business, anyway.

The FBI man had a newspaper under his arm, and he sat down on the bench with Durell and pretended to read it. "No luck, Sam."

"They got through the roadblocks?"

"We found the Cad ditched ten miles up the river. They didn't stay in it long. A couple of kids in a beat-up Ford were hauled out of their car and slugged to a pulp. They're in a hospital. The Ford was used to get to Fremont, thirty miles from here. They got through all the roadblocks, all right. You know how?"

"Tell me," Durell said.

"They ditched the Ford near a swamper's shack and forced the old Cajun in it to take them by pirogue through the bayous. There are enough fingers of water in there for an army to slip through unseen from the roads."

73

"I know," Durell said.

"The sheriff did his best. My office is sending out a six-state alarm. The whole district has been alerted. The swamper told us where he was finally released. On the main highway, so they're either in New Orleans this minute, or on their way out of the state altogether."

"They might have split up," Durell suggested.

"That won't make the job any easier." MacCreedy paused. "The swamper is in the hospital, too. They beat him up as a token of thanks for his help. Tibault is in the hospital, too. Those boys have a taste for violence all their own."

"It's Slago," Durell said. "I had a good look at him. Did you talk to the bank people about the robbery?"

"I've got nothing you don't know already. Everybody inside just keeled over with no warning. No smell, no taste, no trace of the gas. No ill effects afterward, luckily. We've issued bulletins to all banks in the area to discontinue their air conditioning until further notice, and to take immediate steps to protect the inlet air ducts one way or another."

Durell nodded. He heard thunder rumbling in the distance, and knew that a Gulf squall was coming across the delta toward the town. The air felt oppressive. Sweat ran down his chest under his shirt.

HE WENT back to his grandfather's steamboat to pack; there was nothing more he could do here. He had had them in his hands, and they had slipped away. Because of Angelina, he reminded himself. McFee would have his hide if he knew he had gone soft back there at Moon's and chose Angelina's safety over hailing these people. You don't risk success because of human weakness. You're not supposed to remember the sweet taste of a girl's lips or the wild exaltations of first love.

Slago would have taken Angelina in the car as a hostage, and afterward, Slago would have killed her. Was he supposed to have risked that for the chance of stopping them at Moon's? He had made his choice and diverted their attention to give Angelina a chance to break free. She was safe, but he had let them escape.

"Samuel?"

His grandfather stood on the wind bridge beside the pilothouse. His hair looked sharply white against the dark thunderheads in the sky. Durell went aboard and walked through the salon of the old sidewheeler, with its dusty plush draperies and Victorian elegance fading from gilt to peeling decay. Jonathan met him on the bridge.

"Are you all right, son? Angelina is here." His eyes were anxious. "She told me what happened at Moon's. You lost your throw, eh?"

"Yes, Grandpa."

"Because of her?"

"Yes."

"Is it bad?"

"Bad enough. I feel as if I've let a plague germ loose. That's what it's like, and I don't know where it will hit next. It wasn't my job to stop them—just to find out where they're going. But I've got a feeling it's going to be bad." Durell felt the warmth of his love for his grandfather. "I'm sorry, but I've got to cut this visit short. I'm going back to Washington."

"I expected that. Angelina is going with you."

"No," Durell said.

"Then you'd better talk fast to her. She's waiting in your cabin and she's made up her mind, and she's the kind of woman it isn't easy to argue with."

"I'll talk to her, Grandpa."

"She was never in love with Pete Labouisse, Samuel. She's always been in love with you. She tells me you saved her life today. But that ain't what drives her. She's a strange woman, more like a man in some ways. She's tough and she's loyal; she won't forget what she owes a man, even to Pete, no matter what she really feels in her heart. She'll go with you. She's made it her business, now."

Durell went down the ladder to the cabin deck and walked down the corridor to the room he had used as a boy. The old steamboat was full of restless sounds. A wind had come up, thrashing and stumbling through the bayou like an uncertain drunk, lurching in from the Gulf. Even though the sidewheeler was secure in the mud, her ancient sides trembled under the irregular pressures of the wind.

ANGELINA was lying on his bed when he entered the cabin. Lightning flickered beyond the big square windows and touched everything with a blue light for a moment. The crash of thunder that followed shook the deck underfoot. He saw two new suitcases on the floor beside his own.

"Angelina?"

She opened her eyes and looked at him and sat up. She wore a light cotton traveling suit that hugged the full, womanly lines of her body. She looked exciting under the tight-fitting suit. But he didn't like the look in her fine, dark eyes.

"Are you going back to Washington, Sam?"

"Yes. What do you think you're doing here?"

"They got away, didn't they? I knew they would."

"Answer me."

"I guess your grandfather has already told you. I closed my store, Sam. I'm going with you and I'm going to find those men."

"Why?"

"Because of what they did to Pete. I can't forget it."

"You can't help me," he said flatly. "You'll only get in my way and make things tougher for me. Will you please stay here?"

"No, I won't. You'll see. Don't argue. Please, please. Nothing is going to change my mind." She lifted her skirt and he saw the smooth tan of her thigh. She took a long Bowie knife, an antique that was sharpened to the keen edge of a razor, and weighed it in her hand. The blade glittered strangely in the light from the coming thunderstorm. "I can use this, Sam. I'm going to. The same way it was used on Pete."

"So you'll do to Slago what was done to Pete?" he asked sharply. "To be like Slago? Is that what you want to become?"

"Maybe."

"But you can't help," he said. "And you're safe here. Those men won't come back to the bayous again. They're not worried about your identifying them, because they don't expect to operate around here again. I don't know where they are now, Angelina. They got away, probably heading north, but it's a big country and it's going to take a lot of men and teamwork to track them down again. What can you do? I've got my own job to take care of. You'd only be in my way."

She shook her head. "I'm going, with you or without you. I can find them."

"How?"

She stood up and put the Bowie knife away, held by

76

elastic high inside her thigh. All her movements were lithe and graceful. She looked at his tall figure in the cabin doorway and then looked down again, her long lashes hiding her eyes. She was part of her environment, Durell thought, a huntress, with a primitive code and an earthy sense of justice. Her father had taught her the Bible since she could understand the spoken word. An eye for an eye . . .

"Listen to me, Sam," she said quietly. "Maybe you'll be angry for what I've done, but I can't help it. I think you'll get over it. We understand each other, don't we? Nobody knows me better than you. And I think I know you, too. We're not children now, and you haven't forgotten how it was. I can't lie to you, Sam. I don't feel any differently now than I did long ago, about you. I know it's different with you, but you don't have to worry about that part of it."

"I know their names." She ticked them off on her fingers. "Mark Fleming and Hugo Slago—he's the one with the knife—and a couple named Corbin. I got that much from Pete, when I found him in the pirogue. I'm sorry I lied to you and told you he hadn't been able to say anything. He told me a little bit, and I didn't know your part in this, so I kept it to myself. I'm not stupid, Sam. I know it all goes back to whatever Pete took when he was in Germany. It's something important, but I don't care about that, I just care what happened to Pete. It's something I've got to do myself, for his sake. He was going to marry me, and I was happy enough about it, I guess, even if I didn't love him the way I ought to. But I can't leave it to the sheriff's men, or that MacCreedy fellow, or to you and the people you work for. Not to strangers. It's my job, mine alone. And I've already asked some questions."

"Where?"

"In New Orleans. I asked about Fleming and Slago. I telephoned after you left me, after Moon's this afternoon. You know what this country is like, Sam. Wide open for all the rackets. Maybe you think now that we're all simple, unsophisticated people. But the rackets came down here, even into the swamps. Every slot machine in the bars, every gambling joint that hides behind a roadside café, every bottle of liquor run in from Cuba without a tax stamp, is worked out of New Orleans. I know some of those men pretty well. I've done favors for them, sometimes, when it paid me to do them favors. Does that surprise you?"

"No," he said. "I guess not."

Angelina said simply: "I'm pretty important around Peche Rouge. "I think I'm the richest woman around here, with Papa's store in my hands. I've made a lot of money and I've got investments the sheriff might not like. Profitable investments, Sam. A lot of men owe me a lot, so when I called some names in the city, I got some answers. I know more about Fleming and Slago than you think. I know where to start looking for them, where they began and where they're likely to end. I'm going north, and I'll ask more questions there."

"I can't let you do that," Durell said.

"You can't stop me."

"You'll only interfere with my work."

"How? By asking my questions in the wrong places, perhaps, and warning them off? We can solve that, Sam. We can go together. If we do that, I promise I won't step out of line. I promise I'll do as you say and not spoil anything for you."

Durell lit a cigarette and looked at her. He knew her well enough to realize he couldn't change her mind. But for all her skill, Angelina would be lost, an easy victim to their violence.

Thunder crashed outside, and he heard the quick patter of rain on the deck overhead. The girl moved close to him.

"Are you angry with me, Sam?"

"No. Just a little surprised about your knife."

"I have more surprises for you," she said softly. "If you will only accept them."

Chapter Ten

THERE was something wrong with Slago, something crazy. Mark feared him because he could not understand it, although he kept a grip on himself and operated smoothly and efficiently. Getting them all out of Louisiana safely with the loot, slipping past the cops and heading north out of the area, was his business. He was in his element, and for the time being nobody questioned his command. Not even Slago. If Mark had had his way, he would have thrown Slago to the cops. Killed him and left him for the crumby sheriff to worry over. But Jessie said they still needed him. And he found it easy to listen to Jessie when she made suggestions.

They had split up in New Orleans. Corbin and Jessie had taken a plane north to Milwaukee. Slago and Mark took a bus to Mobile, and from there they drove north in a second-hand car Mark bought with some of the bank money. He sold the car in Louisville and they flew from Kentucky to rendezvous in New York with the Corbins at their old apartment. The escape took three days. Once out of Louisiana, the ripple of excitement caused by the bank operation had gradually died. They had had no trouble. It was easy to lose yourself in the country, if you knew where to go. For the most part, the cops were not alert enough to be even looking for them, and Fleming began to feel they didn't even have a decent description. The girl had kept her mouth shut, back in Peche Rouge, but he couldn't guess why. Slago was Mark's biggest worry.

He was alternately sullen, drinking silently and heavily; or he was loud and abusive. There was a queer glitter in his eyes that never quite went away, no matter what mood he was in.

Mark was cautious enough not to pin the whole blame on Slago for what had happened at the fishing camp. Slago was like an unexploded bomb, ready to go off if you touched the wrong piece of mechanism. So Mark left him strictly alone. He felt it was Slago's fault the girl had spotted them when they cracked the bank. And he knew that Slago was wrong in wanting to go on to another bank now. For a few hours, back there, everything seemed to have blown up.

It was Durell, Mark thought. They should have been on the watch for him, since Peche Rouge was his home town, too. He had rightfully belonged on the list from the start. Slago had remembered about him, as far back as Indiana, and had wanted to look into him. The Cajun had acted like a cop back there at Moon's, and Mark wished he knew more about Durell. He didn't like the way he had shown up like that, breaking up the operation. Since Durell had been with G-2 back in Germany, it made sense to suppose he had gone on being a cop of some kind. Maybe he was working locally out of the sheriff's office in the bayou parish. Maybe. Mark still felt uneasy about him, wondering how much Durell might piece together out of the past, remembering how close he had brought them to disaster back there at the fishing camp.

The meet in New York took place without trouble. Nobody was looking for them up North. Mark and Slago checked into a midtown hotel on Forty-seventh Street. It was a sleazy place, occupied by transients and unemployed actors, and the sort of permanent resident who finds a dark hole in the middle of the teeming city and hides in it for uncounted years, unnoticed and unmourned when they go. Mark and Slago checked it at four P.M. on Tuesday, and he started to call the Corbin apartment as soon as he dropped his bag and locked the door.

Slago went to the window and looked sullenly at the crowded street below. "This the best we can do, with all the dough?" He scowled at Mark, his head thrust forward on his thick shoulders. "I thought we were going to stay down South and knock off a whole row of hick banks."

"This is the best place for us now," Mark said. "Thanks to that girl."

"So what do we do, settle for the dimes we took?"

"Jessie will know what to do. Now shut up and let me call her."

Slago's eyes glittered. "You still think I goofed, huh? You think I shoulda sliced the girl?"

"No. As far as we know, she hasn't described us to the cops, and nobody has an idea who we are. Forget it."

"And Durell?" Slago sneered. "You had a gun on him and he took it from you like you were a kid playing Hopalong."

"We both made mistakes," Mark said wearily. "Let's drop it."

"All right, call her. But I don't take orders from a dame."

J ESSIE answered the phone on the second ring. She sounded cool. "We've been here since morning," she told Mark. "But I don't think it will be wise for Erich

80

and me to remain long. I have a feeling we might be tagged here."

"You could move in with us," Mark said. "Are you okay?"

"There was no trouble on the trip."

"I want to see you," Mark said. "Alone."

"Erich wants to discuss the next step."

"To hell with Erich. I want to see you. Just the two of us."

"Mark, don't be unreasonable. It's important that we all work together. We're not checked because of a little trouble. That's not vital. The main thing is that Erich was right, and everything worked fine."

"Except that the cops may be onto us now," he said bitterly.

"That won't matter. We'll begin our next move tomorrow. We won't sit still and wait for them to pick us off. Be reasonable, darling. Don't make any trouble now."

"Alone," he said stubbornly. "Right away."

He heard her sigh on the telephone. "All right, I'll send Erich out. Come over in twenty minutes."

Mark hung up. Slago was still at the window. "What's so important, you've got to get cozy with her?"

Mark didn't reply. He found it best to ignore Slago lately. The sound of Jessie's voice had stirred him, and all at once he felt confident and optimistic that things would work out. He looked at himself in the mirror and straightened his tie. He still looked sharp. A little tired, but good. Jessie knew what he wanted. He had asked, and she had agreed. The thought of seeing her alone . . . Then Slago suddenly put a brutal hand on his shoulder and spun him around.

"All right, Mark, spit it out. What's on buddy boy's sneaking mind? You cutting me out? You making a play for the girl to cut me out?"

"Don't be a fool."

"Then why alone?"

"You think I want to put on a peep show?" Mark smiled.

"Smart bastard. She isn't putting out for you."

"We'll see," Mark said.

"You're fixing a deal with her, buddy boy, to cut me out."

"You're stupid," Mark said flatly. "We've only started. So the bank was for dimes. So maybe the other banks

81

are going to smarten up. But she's got a deal. She's got a place in mind. Like Fort Knox, she said. Until we get Erich to make us a supply of the gas, we play cozy. I see her alone. I get to her once, Slago, and she's around my little finger."

"You think you've got that much," Slago said.

"I can teach her a thing or two. All I need is the first time, just once. Then you and I don't need the Corbins, once we learn the place where all the loot is, and a supply of Erich's gas."

Slago stepped back to the window. His big arms swung loosely at his sides, his head was thrust forward. He looked like a puzzled gorilla.

"I don't trust you, Mark. You cross me, and I kill you."

"Don't worry about a thing," Mark said.

MARK liked being back in New York. He liked the asphalt heat of the streets, the excitement in the air—the crowds, the taxis, the traffic. Some day he would own it all.

The apartment was on the second floor of a private brownstone in the East Seventies, with a black wrought-iron rail on the steps, a brass carriage lantern polished and gleaming against the bright red door, and antique number plates above. He rang the bell and waited and wondered what the apartment cost per month, and when the buzzer clicked he went on up quickly, two steps at a time until he was close to the top of the carpeted stairs, where he slowed to a deliberately casual walk.

Jessie wore a cool print frock of lime green. Her hair looked different. She had cut it, and it looked like one of those Italian deals, like a boy. It made her seem taller, and her whole look revived the quick excitement in him.

"Baby."

"Come in, Mark. Erich has gone, but we won't have much time. We have a lot to talk about. Let's get the business out of the way, shall we?"

"We can talk business later," Mark said. "Do you have any idea how it's been with me, since that last time?"

"Mark, I thought you were tough and intelligent. There will be time to play later, time enough for you and me, just the two of us. Right now we have work to do."

"You said Erich will be back soon."

"There will be a few minutes."

"Who likes to rush?" he said, grinning.

She laughed. "You're hopeless."

"I'm crazy about you."

"And you can have me," she said quietly. "I feel the same way, believe me. But not right now. Come here, Mark." She took his hand and led him through the octagonal foyer into the huge living room. It was quiet and hushed and rich and elegant, remote from the teeming city outdoors. He felt a moment's awe. "Sit down, Mark. You see, I've been working all the time. Look at these."

There was a library table against one wall, and it was covered with rolls of blueprints and tracing paper. He preferred to watch Jessie as she walked toward the couch and sat down with him.

"Give me a cigarette and tell me how you made out, first," she said. "You had no trouble with the police?"

"No trouble all the way."

"This Durell. Have you thought about him?"

"I think he's a local cop, or something, down there. I don't think we have to worry about him." Mark said.

"But I do worry. It's smart to worry."

"Yes," he said. "You're smart—beautiful and smart. That's what makes me do this," he said, and he touched her. She didn't move away. She leaned a little closer to him. "You understand?" he said. "I don't give a damn about anything except you, Jessie. You're like a fever in me."

"You've got to think straight. I'm counting on you, Mark."

"I can't, baby."

She sighed in exasperation. "Will you listen to me? Will you listen for just a few minutes, before Erich gets back? Our next step is all worked out. We need Erich and we need Slago, but in two days—maybe three—we won't need either of them again."

He listened now.

"We'll have all the money we'll ever want, Mark. We'll have it made. I've even bought our airline tickets to Buenos Aires. For just the two of us. Can't you wait that long, darling?"

"No," he said. "What do we do with Erich and Slago?"

She shrugged. "You'll have to get rid of them."

"For good?"

"Why not?"

Mark admired her. "I like that. And I want to know

83

what the operation is about, all right. But you can tell me later."

"You'll do exactly as I say? Promise? Everything I tell you to do? You won't argue about it, or get stiff-necked or anything because I'll give the orders?"

"Not until it's all over."

"You promise, Mark?"

"Sure."

"Please," she said. "I can take it off myself."

She stood up and loosened a catch or two and her dress fell with soft rustlings to her feet. Her body gleamed in the dim, curtained room, her image reflected again and again in diminishing curves in the two huge mirrors that faced each other from opposite walls. Mark reached for her and she smiled. He thought her eyes looked odd as she looked down at him, but he dismissed the thought and the sliding uneasiness it brought him.

Somebody knocked impatiently on the door.

"Wait," she whispered. "It's Erich."

"That bastard will—"

"Stay right here. Please."

She walked through the foyer, as naked as the Greek statuette he could see on its black pedestal, and then she slid the bolt aside and opened the door slightly. Mark could see it was Erich in the hall, holding a paper bag of something that she must have told him to buy. Erich could see him, too. But the man's eyes were on his wife's body.

"Erich, take it back. Take a long walk. Don't hurry."

The man sounded as if he were strangling. "Jessie, you're my—"

"I'm nothing to you. Do as I say."

She shut the door in Erich's white face, bolted it, and walked back, smiling, to where Mark waited for her.

Chapter Eleven

EARLIER that day, in the morning, Durell returned to the Waggonner Building off Fourteenth Street in Washington. The blonde typist with the jeweled harle-

84

quin glasses sat at the same desk and, for all Durell knew, she was typing the same letter. The rack of uniforms that represented the manufacturing company of McGuire, Sloan & Levy were now all air force blues.

A thin rain was falling, but Mr. Wittington still wore his rumpled seersucker suit. His thin face was impassive as he waved Durell to a chair and then lifted his hand to smooth imaginary hair on his bald scalp. Kincaid stood by the window, looking young and military.

Wittington did the talking. "MacCreedy won't get anywhere, Durell. It may seem to you like a job for organization, the sort of thing the FBI does very well, indeed. But they won't find Erich Corbin."

"My fault," Durell said. "I almost had them."

"Just as well you didn't take them. You see, we—our Special Bureau—do not want them in custody yet. That is not our affair."

"They're murderers," Durell said.

Wittington fanned the air. "Only incidental."

"Not to the people who were murdered." Durell said. "If MacCreedy can pick them up—"

"We know where Corbin is. MacCreedy does not. For your information, they're in New York. Back at their former apartment, and obviously feeling safe and secure. Nobody knows this except our man who spotted them and we three in this room. They are not to be intercepted, interrogated, or interfered with." Mr. Wittington leaned forward, his thin shoulders hunched in his seersucker suit. His bald head gleamed. "Do you know why, Durell? Because we still don't know what Erich Corbin is after. It's not the small pickings of a few bank robberies. We're fairly certain of that. It's something bigger. Much bigger. I have a very dissatisfied feeling in my bones, Durell. I don't like it at all. It is my feeling— and for once the machine Mr. Kincaid relies upon now backs me up—my feeling is that the bank robbery in Peche Rouge was nothing, a mere trial, on a small scale, for something bigger. We don't know what it is. And we must find what it is before it happens. If we pull in Corbin, he won't talk. And if we pull in Fleming or Slago, they won't talk, because the chances are that Corbin hasn't told them yet."

"Then why did they tip their hands with the Peche Rouge bank?"

"It is also my feeling that Corbin felt it necessary to

85

convince his partners that his gas operated successfully. It was nothing more than a calculated risk. So far as he knows, it worked fine."

"They have the formula now. And the antidote. I didn't stop them from finding it."

"No fault of yours. We sent you down there too late." Wittington looked up as Kincaid made a vague sound. "Something troublesome, Daniel?"

"I want to know about the girl," Kincaid said. "This Angelina Greene who came up here with Durell."

"She's in my apartment now," Durell said.

"And busy making telephone calls to all sorts of underworld associates, apparently." Kincaid looked angry. "Why did you bring her?"

"To know what she's up to. Short of taking her into custody, she can't be stopped from carrying out her plan for revenge. You have to understand the bayou people—"

Wittington interrupted. "We know all that. I approve."

"I didn't know I was under surveillance." Durell said. "I didn't know you bugged my telephone."

"Do you object?"

Durell shrugged. "No. It's a sort of occupational hazard. I brought the girl with me to keep in touch with her activities. It was either that, or jail her. And she may turn up something useful. If she does, I'll be right on top of it."

"Is that your only reason for bringing her?" Kincaid asked.

Durell was angry. "I knew her a long time ago."

"Intimately," Kincaid said.

"Then you know all about that, too."

"Everything," Kincaid said. "And I don't like it."

Wittington made another pass at his imaginary mane of hair. "Never mind. Daniel, you worry too much. Durell can handle her. It may be for the best, as he says." He stood up, glared at the rain-dotted window as if the weather were a personal affront, and said: "Take her with you to New York, Durell. Understand, you're not to worry Corbin or his people. Not until you find out what his next move is to be."

"Any suggestions?" Durell asked.

"You might meet them. After all, they know you saw them at that fishing camp. You might try to join them. It's up to you. Just take care of yourself."

"But I can't touch them?"

86

"They need more rope. And you don't tell MacCreedy or his New York people. They have jurisdiction and they might move in anyway, but then we'll never learn what Corbin is after." Wittington went to the door and paused. "It isn't Corbin who worries me. It's his objective. Whatever it is, it is an obvious weak spot that he feels he can crack with this nerve gas of his. We don't know the objective and can't guess at the weak spot. If we stop him, we may never know. And we must find out. We've got to plug all the gaps in our armor, Durell. Corbin may fail through overanxiety on our part to check him, but then somebody else may try. And we may never know about *that* one until it is too late."

H IS apartment was on a quiet side street not far from Rock Creek Park. It was raining harder when Durell paid off his taxi and walked to the entrance. The furnishings in his room were simple and utilitarian; a leather armchair and couch, a heavy desk with a three-spot lamp over it, books in a low bookcase under the windows. Deirdre had brought over the paintings on the wall and had bought the curtains and helped furnish the bedroom.

He heard Angelina when he unlocked the door, and when he came in he saw her put down the telephone. She wore a small visored hat tilted back on her dark hair, and a transparent raincoat belted over a gabardine suit of pale blue. She looked lovely and smart and very unlike the girl in denims and shirt in the bayou country. She could have appeared anywhere and been accepted everywhere.

"Sam," she said, "you were not gone very long."

"Who were you talking to?"

"A man who knows somebody named Big Socks Johnson, who is a minor executive of the syndicate, and who employed Mark Fleming until a couple of months ago."

"You get around."

"I told you, I have contacts. My investments—"

"What did the man who knows the man tell you?"

"Mark Fleming is in New York, with Slago, at the Belmont on West Forty-seventh Street."

He looked at the small, smart traveling case near the door. "Were you ready to go there now? Did I come back too soon?"

"I was going to wait for you, but I am going there."

"You'll get yourself killed," he said.

"Then come with me."

"I intend to. Could we have some coffee first?"

"I don't like the kind of coffee they drink up here."

"You'll like mine," Durell said. "Jonathan sends it up to me regularly. It's from home."

"In that case, yes."

He went into the kitchen and started water boiling in the coffee pot and wondered wryly why Mr. Wittington didn't have as much information as Angelina had obtained with her telephone calls. Perhaps it wasn't quite that simple, though. He was impressed with the girl, not just with what she had learned, but with the way she looked and the way she was. He wondered if the Bowie knife strapped to her thigh troubled her when she walked. He heard her come into the kitchen and looked at her. She had taken off her white gloves and the cute hat, and he watched her get coffee mugs from the cupboard.

"Sam?" She spoke with her back to him. "Don't you find it strange, our being together again, the way we used to be?"

"It's not quite the way it used to be," he pointed out.

"Well, that's not my fault."

"I know."

She said down at the kitchen table. "Who is Deirdre Padgett?'

"My girl."

"Are you going to marry her?"

"I don't know."

"But if she's your girl, and if you've known her long—"

"A couple of years."

"But you haven't married her?"

"No. How did you learn her name?"

"She telephoned from Paris, about an hour ago." Angelina grinned, but her eyes were dark and somber. "Don't worry; I explained who I was."

"That wouldn't be any help."

"I told her I was here purely on business."

"I'll bet."

"Are you angry with me?"

"No."

"And you're really in love with her?"

"Yes."

"Then why is she in Paris?"

"That's a good question." Durell told her about Deirdre's job as a fashion editor with a Washington newspaper. He couldn't explain why they had never married. He couldn't tell her it was his fault, that if there was anything in the world he feared, it was hurting Deirdre; in his business it was better not to have permanent arrangements that caused someone to love you too much. Deirdre had always had other arguments to counter this, but she had not yet shaken him and he was beginning to believe she never would.

"Sam, what is your job?" Angelina asked suddenly. "I mean, just what do you *do?*"

"I'm with the government."

"Are you a G-man?"

He laughed, becaused she sounded naive. "No."

"But you're a cop of some kind?"

"Of some kind, yes."

"Your job is to get Corbin and Fleming and Slago, isn't it."

"My job is to get them at the right time and the right place, and not before, and if you do anything to throw a monkey wrench into this thing, I'll have to—" He paused.

She smiled. "What, Sam?"

"I'll treat you as if you were one of them," he said flatly.

Her smile was erased as if by a sponge. She took a sudden, shaken breath, "I think you mean that," she whispered wonderingly.

"I do."

"No wonder this Deirdre is in Paris."

He poured coffee and drank it and enjoyed the chicory flavor of the Louisiana blend. Angelina stared at her folded hands on the table. "Sam, haven't you ever thought about me in all these years?"

"Yes, quite often."

"But there's nothing left for us, is there?"

"I honestly don't know."

"Don't you want to find out? We have time right now. Or are you afraid?"

"I've got a job to do," he said. He grinned. "And you've got a sharp knife there."

Her face was pale. "Damn you. Do you have to remind me?"

"I'm sorry."

"Sam, if I told you now that I still love you, and always have, and that I would give anything to you—if you believed that, Sam, and then I spoiled this job you have to do, would you do that thing to me, as you said?"

"Yes, Angelina."

She looked at him without understanding.

Chapter Twelve

B Y THREE o'clock that afternoon, Durell was in New York. He took a room across the street from the house in the East Seventies, and from the window he could see Corbin's elegant doorway, with its shiny brass knocker and antique house numbers. There was nothing so elaborate in the house where Durell found the room. His window was diagonally opposite the Corbin apartment, and the house was just an old, shabby rooming house, not reconditioned and refurbished as Corbin's was.

It was still raining in New York when he had arrived with Angelina, who insisted on sharing the room with him.

"There's not much privacy," he said.

"I don't want privacy."

"It's blackmail," he said. "You know that, don't you?"

She smiled, taking off the white visored hat, setting down her grip, shaking rain from her raincoat. "Yes, Sam."

"Promise me something, then."

"Of course, Sam."

"Don't do anything. Just stay here with me. Don't call your underworld friends about your investments, and don't go playing cops and robbers on your own. Forget about your revenge."

"To everything you ask, yes, except the last. I can't forget Pete."

"Then make yourself comfortable. We may have a long wait."

He watched Corbin's house from behind the thin curtains in the bay window. Now and then he heard Angelina move about, unpacking, testing the big double bed. The street was an ordinary crosstown street, with small maples struggling uneasily in the midsummer rain. Between five and six o'clock the number of pedestrians increased. Two men appeared, walking dogs. Some cabs stopped at various houses, and men got out and went into the smug, smart doorways across the sidewalk. They lived in a different world from the men who lived on this side of the street. But that's the way it is in New York, Durell thought; twenty paces, and you're in a different world.

He didn't see Erich or Slago. Nobody came out of the house with the red doorway.

"Sam, may I go out and get some food?" Angelina asked. "There's a hot-plate here, and I could do a little cooking."

He had to admit he was hungry. "Be careful. Don't let them see your face from their windows."

"Naturally. I won't be long."

He watched her leave and then he watched from the window again. He knew how to do this. He could have stayed at the window all night, all the next day, perhaps for a week. He had been trained in patience, in watchfulness, in waiting. But he didn't intend to wait forever.

It continued to rain. He saw that the house he watched was generally quiet, with only one couple entering the red doorway during the time Angelina was gone. There was a high iron picket rail around the top of the roof, and this interested him, because the rail and the potted, stunted orange trees up there indicated a roof garden or a terrace. And this in turn indicated a reasonably accessible entrance from the roof.

Finally he saw Erich come down the street from Madison Avenue. The gray-haired man seemed to walk awkwardly, paused, wrung his hands as he stood on the steps, started to go in, changed his mind, returned to the sidewalk, and looked up at the second-floor windows. He stood there a few minutes, not heeding the rain, and then turned and walked rapidly back the way he had come.

Durell found this very interesting.

A few minutes later a green Buick station wagon came around the corner and double-parked in front of the house. Slago got out and also stood for a moment in the rain. Erich returned from the corner and the two men talked, with Slago making angry gestures. Erich used his hands placatingly. Then both men walked around to the back of the station wagon and looked inside. Durell wished he could see what they were looking at. Then Corbin and Slago got into the station wagon and drove away. Durell made a note of the license number.

He wished Angelina would come back.

She had been gone over half an hour. He felt uneasy. He told himself that actually he knew very little about her. What had happened between them had been when they were practically children. Puppy love, that had expressed itself in the practical, earthy terms of the bayou people. There had been inhibitions between them. Her body had been ripe then, as now, and ready for love, generous in her giving, just as she would be generous now if he gave her a sign that he wanted her. She was simple, yet devious; a woman at sixteen, full of a wildness that had enchanted and alarmed him. Even then, he remembered, she had been ambitious and clever at making money in her father's store. How many men had she loved since those days? Where had her wild ambition actually taken her? He knew she had traveled devious paths, touching the edges of the dark labyrinth of the underworld, making money from it all, learning to be self-sufficient and strong. How much of her reason for being here sprang to a primitive, native instinct for vengeance; and how much was for some more obscure reason he hadn't yet fathomed? He didn't know. He only wished she would come back soon.

He was not in love with her any more. He was in love with Deirdre. It didn't matter that Deirdre was in Paris today, and Angelina was here with him now. Angelina had nothing he could accept.

Forty-five minutes had passed, and she hadn't returned.

THE DOOR to Corbin's house opened and Mark Fleming and Jessie came outside into the evening rain. They were laughing at something Mark said, and they held hands, and even at this distance, they looked like lovers, the way they walked and touched each other. They waited on the sidewalk, and after a minute a cruising cab stopped and they both got in and the cab turned south on Madison.

The apartment was now empty.

Durell waited a minute or two longer for Angelina, and then he couldn't wait any longer. He left his window and quit the shabby room and walked outside. The rain was light and warm and gentle. The street lights came on, although it was still an hour before true dusk. He had a rented car parked around the corner, and he would have followed his quarry if it had looked as if they were leaving for good. But there was every indication that they felt secure enough to come back to this place. There might be time enough now to make a quick survey of the rooms over there and see what he could turn up.

The street door was locked, and he did not want to arouse the other tenants by pushing any bell at random, so he tried the next house. He rang two bells and when the buzzer buzzed, he stepped into the small foyer. A woman looked at him from a first-floor doorway and at the same time a man's voice called down from above. He said, "Excuse me, wrong bell," to the woman and went upstairs. The man had called from the third floor. Durell waited on the second landing until he heard a door slam in exasperation above, then he kept going noiselessly up to the fifth and top floor. A door opened easily onto the roof from here.

There was a high iron fence between the two roofs, and it took some precarious moments while he swung around the back end, hovering for a second or two over the courtyards far below. Then he was on the roof of the Corbin house. The door going down was locked, but he took a flat leather case from his pocket and manipulated several pieces of flat steel in the lock, finally getting inside. He drifted silently down to the second floor and repeated his manipulations with the lock-picks on Corbin's door, and in a few moments he was where he wanted to be.

No lamps had been left on, but enough light shone through the windows from the street to show him the way. He saw the high-ceilinged elegance of the living room and the long baroque table with its blueprints, and he touched the rolls tentatively, then turned down a wide hallway with a tesselated floor, passed a window-less kitchen, and entered the huge bedroom at the rear. A low balcony, under which were situated double baths and wardrobe rooms, occupied the inner end of the

93

bedroom. Durell paused in the gloom, noting the rumpled condition of the bed, a big bath towel on the floor, the repetition of mirrors on the pilastered walls. Suitcases stood on a luggage rack near the windows, but they were closed and locked and he knew he might leave a scar on the leather if he forced them open.

He was not sure what to look for. Wittington wanted to give them rope enough to find out where they had seen the flaw in the nation's defenses. Maybe it had nothing to do with defense or national security, however. Maybe it was strictly a criminal operation. He didn't know, and that was what he had to find out.

He wondered if Angelina had returned to the room.

He began searching the bedroom, swiftly and methodically. Jessie Corbin's clothing had expensive labels and reflected a European flare for style. He knew very little about her. The dossier that Wittington had given him at the Special Bureau office had mentioned a Midwestern farm background, college at Des Moines, a frustrated year trying to break into the Broadway theater, and then some years abroad with dubious liaisons throughout Europe. Durell wished he knew what she wanted. She had married a man twenty years older than herself. Not for love; not a woman like this. Not even for money. Corbin was a refugee, a man in flight. Then where had the money come from to rent this place, to buy these clothes? There was nothing here to tell him.

He gave up the bedroom and checked the baths, noting the Spartan simplicity of Erich Corbin's possessions as opposed to his wife's taste for luxury. An odd couple. He remembered how Jessie had looked leaving the apartment with Fleming. Something interesting there. Did Erich condone it? The rumpled bed told an interesting story. Who gave the orders in this strange group?

He returned to the living room. The street was dark and quiet now. A cab went by, tires hissing on the wet asphalt. It was an ordinary, peaceful, residential street. He could see the window of the room he had rented diagonally across the way. No light shone there. He began to feel it had been a mistake to let Angelina go. He didn't quite trust her.

H E CHECKED the blueprints on the baroque table. He wished he could risk a light, but he respected Corbin's intelligence. Jessie, too, would know if she had left a light on and if she returned too soon and saw the windows bright, she would be warned. He took the blueprints to the window and tried to make something of the complicated pattern by the light of the street lamp. They were air-conditioning plans for a vast and complex structure on many levels, but there were no labels to give him the slightest hint of what this place was or what its function might be. Whatever it was, it was big and important. It vindicated Wittington's theory that another much bigger target was Corbin's goal.

There was a name in neat, architectural script in the lower corner of the prints. Durell risked a match to read it. *Carl Amberly.* And under it: *Groversville, Penna. August, 1957.*

Durell replaced the rolls on the table exactly as they had been before. There seemed to be nothing else in the apartment to tell him anything. He stood looking at his tall, dim reflection in the mirrors that reflected the room endlessly. He saw frustration in his dark face. His white shirt looked very white, his suit very dark, in the uncertain light. He took out a cigarette, put it into his mouth, and decided not to smoke it and put it away.

Returning to the bedroom, he closed the door and risked a light, which would not show on the street. There was an extension phone beside the bed, and an address and number book in tooled leather. He opened the book and leafed through it and saw the numbers of grocers, tailors, a beauty parlor. No familiar names of associates. But on the back cover, scribbled hastily as if jotted down in a hurry, was another name to go with that of Carl Amberly.

George Johnston. Beside it was, *3 rms, $450 season.* And again: *Groversville, Pa.* He wondered if Johnston was a realty agent.

Excitement moved in him. He had something tangible, something he could work with. He looked at his watch. It was after seven. He wondered if he should call Wittington to put someone to work on these names and places. He would have liked to describe the blueprints in better detail, too. Thinking of this, Durell returned to the living room for the big rolls of heavy paper, then walked back to the telephone. Just as the operator asked his number, he heard a key turn in the front door.

Durell quietly put down the phone. The blueprints were in his hand. There was no chance to return them to the living room now. He stood up and turned off the lamp and went to the bedroom door. He took out his gun.

The front door opened and someone came quietly into the apartment.

Chapter Thirteen

A T SEVEN o'clock Slago backed the station wagon up against the loading platform of a warehouse in lower Brooklyn. Erich sat beside him, leaning slightly forward. Slago was surprised, because he thought Erich was drunk, and he had never seen Erich drink before. There was something on Erich's mind that had nothing to do with their appointment here, and Slago wondered if Mark had made a slip about Jessie. Dames were dames. They were all alike to Slago. He couldn't see why Mark had to mess around with Jessie in particular, when they all had to get along smoothly for the next few days. Slago did not consider himself clever or intelligent. He knew his limitations. He knew what he could and what he could not do, and because of this he operated very efficiently on the levels where he chose to function. His drives were simple and primitive, and because of his simplicity, he often fooled cleverer and subtler men.

He was worried about Erich, because Erich wasn't himself. Erich was usually cold and precise, the Teutonic personality that pushed emotion and irrelevancies aside and stuck to business. Right now, Erich didn't seem to be aware of the job they had to do here.

The warehouse was dark, closed for the night. Slago got out of the car, leaving Corbin wrapped in his cloak of dark thought. The doors on the loading platform were closed, but as he went lightly up the steps, one of them slid aside and a bald man in short-sleeved pink shirt stepped out. He carried a watchman's clock on a leather shoulder strap and a holstered gun.

"You're right on time."

"Have you got what we ordered, buddy boy?" Slago asked.

"Sure thing. Have you the money?"

"I got five hundred for you."

"I had a lot of trouble juggling the books upstairs to cover this on the inventories," the watchman said nervously.

"You said five hundred."

"I know, but—"

"Come on, then, let's roll it out."

The bald man was afraid of Slago, but he stood his ground. "Pay me first."

Slago took the money from his pocket and tossed it to the deck of the loading platform. The watchman licked his lips angrily, but he looked again at Slago's bulk and picked up the money meekly and went inside.

The loading went without difficulty. There were two compressed gas cylinders, dials and instruments to be attached to the nozzles, a dozen boxes of chemicals, and two carboys. The station wagon took it all without difficulty. Slago preferred this Buick to the Cad, which was too flashy for his taste and didn't have the capacity of the station wagon. The watchman was worried and he nodded once to Erich, seated in the car, and said, "Why doesn't your pal help?"

"He's got his troubles."

"Look, I ain't curious, mister, but I'd like to know—"

"No, you don't want to know," Slago said. "You'd be goddam sorry if you knew anything at all, right?"

"Maybe so."

"Damn right. Just forget everything now, huh?"

"Sure. Any time you want to do more business—"

"I'll look you up, don't worry," Slago said. He laughed, a short spurt of gravelly sound, and got back into the Buick. "We've loaded everything, Erich."

"That is fine."

"Don't you want to check it?"

"I trust you. I'm not worried about you, Slago."

"But you're worried about something, huh?" Slago started the car and when the watchman opened the high wire gate he turned on the headlamps because it was getting dark. He headed for the Belt Parkway and the bridges to Manhattan. "You ain't yourself, Erich," he said slyly. "And when a smart guy like you takes a tailspin, it's got to be a dame. It's your broad, isn't it?"

"My wife," Erich said, kneading his hands together.

"There are plenty of other broads around, buddy."

"You don't understand. I love her."

"So she's got something different."

"For me, yes."

"Jesus, you guys kill me. We don't need her, buddy."

Erich looked pale in the intermittent light that came into the car as they drove along the parkway. His nose looked pinched and white. "You still do not understand. We cannot drop her, even if I so desired it. Even if I could bring myself to do it. She humiliates me. She sleeps with Mark, did you know that?"

"Sure," Slago said. "So it costs you something?"

"I would kill her, if I had the true courage. I have been thinking of it all afternoon. She brings mad thoughts to my mind. But we cannot get rid of her, Slago, because it is all her money. She had financed all this. Why? I know she never truly loved me, but she helped me come across the border to the West. She has her own plans, her own goals. Do you know how much she hates this country? She thought she had great talent that was once rejected. She told me one night, in London, how she was given an acting part, a good part in a great show, and then she was kicked out for another actress because the other actress had a man who put money into the production. So she gave it up and left, with her bitterness and her hatred, and she came to Europe. All of this is her idea, Slago. She is after something she will not talk about, but I don't know what it is."

"I thought it was simple," Slago said. "I thought we were all after just one thing—money."

"She wishes for something else."

"And you're sure you don't know what it is?"

"I can guess. I do not want to talk about it."

"Maybe you better talk about it," Slago said.

"She is using Mark. She is using you and me. She is smarter than all three of us together."

"Nobody's smarter than the knife. That cuts 'em all down to fish bait. Keep talking, Erich."

"No, I have said enough."

"You said too much and not enough. Tell me, Erich."

Corbin looked up and saw Slago's face and he remembered who and what Slago was.

At a little before seven, Angelina sat on a stool in the bar of the Belmont Hotel and sipped straight rum from a shot glass. She hoped Durell would not worry about her. She hoped he understood how she felt about Pete, which had very little to do with how she felt about Durell. It was something she owed Pete, she told herself, and it didn't matter that Sam had other ideas about how to handle them. Sipping the rum, she recalled what he had said about abandoning her if she didn't obey his orders. But she couldn't believe he would do this. She knew him too well; she remembered too much about him. Remembering, she smiled, the languid warmth of a bayou afternoon probing deep inside her.

They were here in this ratty hotel, the men who had killed Pete Labouisse. She was not afraid of them. All her life, she had known how to maneuver men to satisfy her own whims. She had given little, actually, and it was not her fault if her face and body promised so much. She had long ago discovered that men always jumped to the same conclusion about her, but they never found out the truth until she had gotten what she wanted from them. And what she had always wanted until now was very simple. She wanted money.

At least, this was what she had wanted until Sam came back. Now she had to admit to a certain amount of confusion. She was still in love with him. For Sam, it was all only a pleasant memory, a warm area of patterns that made him what he was today. But she felt sure she could make him love her again. Once this was over, there would be time. She would make him love her, and then things would be the way they used to be. So if she could hurry things up, instead of just waiting and watching, the way he wanted to do it, then she could settle things sooner.

Angelina finished the rum just as Slago returned to the hotel. He came in alone, moving slowly, and he turned straight to the bar, just as she had hoped he would.

Angelina felt a quickening of tension, but she put the shot glass down with a steady hand, Her face was lovely and serene, reflected in the bar mirror. There were two men at the far end of the bar, arguing about baseball, and a middle-aged woman with a Martini held in a deathgrip in her ringed fingers. Slago took a stool two removed from her and ordered rye and then looked up under his heavy brows and saw her in the mirror.

For a moment nothing changed in his broad, flat face. His brush of salt-and-pepper hair and his big, powerful hands were the things Angelina remembered.

She smiled at him.

He looked at her, and there was a flatness in his eyes that momentarily turned her stomach to jelly. She kept the smile there, working at it, trying hard to get across to him what she wanted. He didn't understand. She saw shock and then disbelief, and then fear and rage, all mirrored fleetingly in those pale eyes in the mirror.

He got up and took the stool next to hers and said in a hoarse whisper: "You're dead, sister."

"Do I look it?" Angelina asked.

"You're fingering me, huh?"

"For the cops? No."

"Where are they?"

"I'm alone. Can't you see that?"

"I believe that. Like the moon is green cheese. They move in now, right now, and you're dead, right here at this bar."

"They're not here. I'm alone. I didn't know whether you'd recognize me or not. We're a long way from where we saw each other last."

Slago wet his lips. His heart still pounded from the shock she had given him by showing up here. He looked at the bartender, but the man was down at the other end of the bar, entering the baseball argument with his two other customers. The woman with the Martini had a drunken fixity in the way she held her glass and stared at nothing. Slago turned his head on his thick neck. He looked into the lobby, he looked through the Venetian slats on the bar window at the dark street. He looked back at Angelina.

"I don't get it."

"I'm here on business."

"What business?"

"We'll talk about that later," Angelina said. "Buy me another drink. Just rum. Cuban, please."

His mouth was open. He was sweating. She had him, he thought. Seeing his confusion, Angelina felt elation until she told herself to be careful, reminding herself that this was the man with the knife, and he had done that thing to Pete, and there was no telling what went on inside that skull of his.

"You saw me at Moon's," Slago said. "I had my hands on you and you got away. Now you're here. How come?"

"I told you. I traced you because of business."

"What business? Who are you?"

"I want to make a deal. May I have that drink, please?"

He didn't understand it. In Slago's world, a woman served only one purpose. You called for them when you needed them, and then you put them aside and forgot them until the next time.

"We'll drink upstairs," he said. He wondered if Mark was back yet. He had left Erich uptown with the station wagon. "We'll talk business, all right." He felt a trembling in his bowels. He put his hand on Angelina's wrist and exerted pressure. Not much. Just enough to hurt her. "Come on, sister."

"My name is Angelina."

"And you're alone," he said flatly.

"That's right. Let go of me."

"Come on."

SHE stood up. He kept his hand on her wrist. She didn't let the pain show through. It wasn't the pain that bothered her. It was the hatred. She didn't know if she could keep it pushed down where he wouldn't see it yet. She wanted to kill him—slowly, the hard way, the way he had killed poor Pete. She didn't want it to come impersonally, from the law. She wanted him to know who was the cause of his death, she wanted him to think about death coming for him. If he knew her as a person, as an individual and not just the blank face of justice, then it would hurt him more and she would be satisfied.

"You don't have to force me," she said quietly.

The pressure on her wrist relaxed a little. Nobody paid any attention to them as they crossed the dingy lobby to the elevator.

Mark wasn't back yet. Slago closed the door, turned the key in the lock, and then, with no warning and no change in his face, he suddenly flung Angelina across the room toward the bed. She stumbled and fell across it, lost her handbag, slid to one knee on the floor, and pulled herself up again.

Slago leaned back against the door. He looked at her legs. "Now, talk."

"Is this the way you always do business?"

"It's the way I do it with you."

Angelina straightened her skirt. One of her nylons had a run in it. She picked up her handbag. He hadn't thought to take her bag away yet. He wouldn't find anything in it, anyway. The knife was still strapped high up inside her thigh, where not even the flare of her skirt as she fell had revealed it.

"You're Slago, aren't you?"

"Keep talking."

"I'm not sure if you're the one I ought to talk to. You're just the muscle. Big Socks told me about you and Fleming. He doesn't know about the Corbins, except that you four are together."

Slago said, surprised: "You know Big Socks Johnson?"

"I've done business with him back home. A sort of sales representative, you might say."

Slago blinked his mean little eyes. "Did he send you?"

"No. I want in. On my own."

"In on what?"

"On what you people have. On how you cracked the bank."

"Why should you get in?"

"Because I know who you are."

"You won't get a chance to talk about it now," Slago said.

"I've already talked. With pen and paper, on a letter to the law. If anything happens to me, if I don't get back to somebody who's waiting for me, the letter goes to the law."

Slago laughed. "That's pure corn."

"It still works."

"So you think you can jack in because you know us?"

"You don't have any choice," Angelina said. "Besides, I can help. Now let's be civilized and have a drink and talk about it."

Slago wished Mark was here. Mark would know what to do with this one. He opened and closed his hands. He made them into hard fists, enjoying the pull of the muscles up his arm. Maybe she was bluffing. She looked cool and smart, though. She was a lush piece. He didn't miss any of that, either. He had heard about the bayou women. This one was smart, but she was only a woman, after all. He made up his mind, watching her take a cigarette from her handbag and light it. The room was quiet. A shabby room in a shabby hotel, filled with people who avoided trouble like the plague.

Angelina saw the change in Slago's face. For a moment it puzzled her. She was sure she had convinced him of two things: that she wasn't fingering him for the police, and that she would carry through her proposal. She watched the way he moved away from the door. His thick shoulders were hunched and his head was pulled into his neck. Something in his eyes looked unnatural.

"Sweetheart, you made a big mistake," Slago said hoarsely. "We ain't stayin' here long enough for any letter of yours to give us any trouble."

"Let's have that drink," Angelina said.

"Shut up and listen. Who sent you? Who's your friend with the letter? Is it that Durell?"

"I just came to talk business in a friendly way," Angelina said. She knew this was all wrong, because she now sounded defensive. All she wanted was for him to busy himself with the bottle. When he wasn't ready, that's when she would do it to him. The shock of the first blow with the knife would make him helpless. After that she would talk to him, tell him who she was and what she intended to do with him. But she took a step backward, toward the bed, and she knew this was wrong, too. "Maybe we'd better wait until Fleming and the Corbins show up," she said.

"You don't think I can handle you, sister?"

"It isn't that. I—"

He slapped her. His move was quicker than she had expected, so quick that the full force of his heavy hand crashed across her cheek and nose. She dropped her handbag. He kicked it aside. He put both hands out and crushed her breasts and pushed her and she fell back on the bed in an agony of pain. She tried to kick at him, but he laughed softly and then he caught her leg and pulled her half off the bed. Her skirt slid up. All the way up.

He saw the Bowie knife strapped to her thigh, and he laughed.

All at once, Angelina knew that this one was different from any other man she had known. And with the knowing, there came a terror that was also different from any fear in the past. She had made a mistake. She had been too sure of herself, certain that Slago was just a man, like any other man when it came to being controlled by a woman. She saw the true blankness in his laughing face, the way his mouth hung open. She tried to get the gleaming Bowie knife.

That was a mistake, too.

His strength was incredible, and he enjoyed using it.

He took the knife from her with an easy twist that sent pain screaming up through the shock of his hand that violated her. She twisted and fell to her knees before him. He had her arm pulled up high behind her then, forcing her head and shoulders down, and he raised his knee and crashed it against her face and then let go of her arm. She fell backward, half under the bed, and tried to crawl away from the screaming pain. She wanted to scream, but she couldn't. Her face felt broken. She felt his hands on her, ripping her clothes away. She felt him pick her up, his fingers digging into her flesh. She bounced on the bed.

"Come on, baby. You wanted to wrestle," he said.

And he said: "Knives are my business, baby."

She saw he had the Bowie knife in his right hand. His left hooked her brassiere, broke it, flung it away. She couldn't breathe. There was a crushing weight on her chest and she saw the ceiling move, fading away into a bright violet shot through with red, a color that wriggled and flooded violently down upon her like a rain of blood. She screamed then, but she didn't hear the sound.

"Who's your friend with the letter? Is it Durell?"

His voice echoed violently inside the dark chamber of her mind. There was no room for it, no room for anything but her panic and the red pain he was inflicting on her. She saw her hands beat against his looming face. Her fists seemed futile, as if they belonged to some stranger, flailing without conscious volition. They were puny against his sullen, maniacal strength. How could she have been so wrong? She should never have left Durell; he had warned her. She had been so sure that her way was right, that they were only men, after all.

Somehow she got out from under him and fell off the bed. Her clothes were in tatters. She got to her hands and knees and looked at her nakedness and saw the bloody pattern on her body and could not believe what she saw. He had used the knife on her. She felt her stomach convulse and then the floor gave way and she slid into darkness that was not darkness, because the red was still there, dark and pulsing, and the sound of his voice moved like fire in it, and then the sound of the door came and another voice moved in with his. . . .

"She's got a friend."

"Who? Did she say?"

"Probably the guy who was with her at Jake Moon's."

"Durell?"

"Who else?"

"What did she want?"

"She wanted to cut in."

"Did you have to do that to her?"

"Ah, she had this knife. She asked for it."

"Damn you, we'll have to get rid of her."

"Uh-uh, buddy boy."

"You've made enough mistakes. We'll get rid of her."

"No, we'll take her along. Maybe that will suck in Durell. The cops aren't in on it. Just the two of them, trying to cut in. That's all, I tell you. I'm sure of it."

"What do you want with her?"

Laughter.

"Look at her. She's too good to waste, buddy."

"I think you're nuts, you know that?"

"Look at her. I'm gonna have some of that. You got Jessie, right? So I'll take some of this."

"The way she is?"

"Jesus, that's the way I like 'em."

Angelina wished she could die. She had expected to deal with men. She knew she had met a monster.

Chapter Fourteen

DURELL stood in the darkness of the Corbin bedroom and listened to the outer door thud softly shut. There was no other way out except a service entrance through the kitchen, and he couldn't reach it without being seen from the foyer. A slab of yellow suddenly showed under the bedroom door as a light in the wall was snapped on. A woman's heels clicked on the tesselated floor, moving toward the front of the apartment, and he opened the bedroom door a crack and looked. He could see Jessie Corbin's straight, slim back for a moment before she moved beyond his range of vision. She had gone straight to the heavy table where he had found the blueprints. Durell looked grimly at the rolls of paper on the bed where he had put them. She had noticed their absence immediately.

His orders were to watch and wait, not to capture. He did not want to be found here, to alarm and alert them and possibly postpone what was being planned. He went to the tall windows in the back of the dark, perfumed bedroom and looked out. A fire escape angled down into the rear courtyard, but the windows were closed, and he doubted if he could raise them without noise.

Then the telephone rang. It rang almost under his hand in the bedroom, and also in the living room. Jessie picked it up on the other extension, and he listened to the quick murmur of the woman's voice. He could see her again from the angle of the bedroom door. It was the best look he'd had of her so far. Her blonde hair was sleek; her face was cold, beautiful, angry, and then thoughful as she listened to the voice in the receiver. Cold fury swept like a gust of wind over her features. Durell turned to the extension beside the bed and lifted it very carefully and listened, too.

". . . have you done with her?" he heard Jessie ask. Mark Fleming's voice replied. "Slago is keeping her." "What for?"

"You know Slago. He thinks he can suck in Durell with her."

Angelina? Durell thought.

Jessie said: "We can't take her with us."

"We've got to."

"Then we should leave at once."

"That's what I was thinking," Mark said.

"No, wait. Just a moment, darling."

Durell held the extension phone and waited. Jessie was silent. She was silent for a long time. He thought, They've got Angelina; She couldn't leave it alone. A coldness spread in him like the creeping of ice through his belly. He had warned her, but she hadn't listened; now he either had to abandon her or go after her, and possibly wreck everything Wittington wanted to achieve.

The silence in the telephone lasted too long. When he looked up, Jessie Corbin stood in the bedroom doorway. She had heard him lift the extension phone. She pointed a gun at him as he stood by the bed with the phone in his hand.

"So you're here," she said. "It didn't take you long." He started to put down the phone.

"Don't," she said. "Be very careful, Mr. Durell."

"I will be."

"Put the phone on the bed. Don't hang up. Step back a bit."

He did as he was told. She handled the gun with a casual grip that told him she was accustomed to guns, and he didn't like that. A gun in a woman's hand was still an unpredictable thing. He stepped back and watched her turn on the light. Her eyes were bright with triumph as she picked up the instrument.

"Mark? Mark, he's right here! I've got him."

Durell could hear the excited clatter of Fleming's voice. He drew a slow, deep breath. Everything had come apart. They knew him. They knew his name. He did not know how much more they knew, but it was too much. For a brief moment, hearing about Angelina, he had lost his caution. He saw the tight smile on the blonde's lips. She was looking at him, and he looked at the black muzzle of the gun pointed at his stomach.

She spoke into the phone. "We'll leave right now. Slago was right. We've got them both. We'll take them with us for a short way . . . Stay on the phone, Mark. Is Erich with you?"

"No. And listen, I'm worried about him. Slago says—"

"Never mind. He's sure to be along soon. Just hang on. When Erich comes, we'll drive over and pick you up with the girl."

"Be careful," Mark said.

"He won't make a move." Jessie looked at Durell. "Not if he wants the girl to live . . . Do you understand?" she asked Durell.

He said nothing, and she took his silence for agreement. There were a few more precise instructions, and then she put down the telephone. She gestured toward a chair. "Sit over there. And tell me why you think we ought to cut you and your girl into the deal. Because you've got a letter she wrote to the police?" Jessie shook her head. "You won't mail it. You don't want Slago to kill her, do you?"

"No," Durell said.

"So you don't go to the police. So you don't cut in."

"If you say so."

Her eyes narrowed with suspicion. Durell knew he was dealing with a quick intelligence. There was an objectivity in the way she looked at him, and lines of frustration around her mouth when she relaxed a little. She didn't care what he thought of her looks. She might be lovely, but not with the gun in her hand. He wondered how much time he had. Corbin was expected at any moment.

He spoke quietly. "You've made a bad mistake, Jessie. You've overlooked something."

"I don't think so. You and the girl are interfering, so we'll get rid of you. It's as simple as that."

"And if I decide to sacrifice the girl now?"

She frowned slightly. "You won't. You're in love with her, aren't you? You wouldn't want Slago to have her."

"I may be in love with her, but I might let Slago have her anyway."

"I doubt that. As an American, you have confused ideas of loyalty, the sanctity of human life, and all those medieval concepts of chivalry that prohibit you from risking the girl to get your own way."

"You sound familiar," Durell said. "You sound like some people I once knew from Moscow."

"I am not a Communist," she said flatly.

"What are you, then? An opportunist?"

"Perhaps."

"Dealing with them?"

"That is nothing to you. You are a small-time operator, Mr. Durell. You saw something you didn't understand, you and your girl, and you tried to muscle in where you don't belong. This was your major error. This, and letting the girl try to work on Slago. She was rather surprised to learn what Slago is. At this moment, Slago is withholding his attentions, but it depends on you."

"Are you going to kill her?"

"Perhaps."

"Isn't there any chance we can join you?"

"We'll talk about it," she said. She paused, eying him. "You said I made a mistake. What is it?"

Durell said: "Thinking I'll sit still for you because of Angelina. You can have her."

He had made up his mind.

He stood up. Her gun moved to follow him. But he knew she wouldn't dare fire in this building. She was too smart for that. He saw the panic of indecision in her eyes. Her gun was a .32 a war-issue Italian Beretta. Loud and noisy, and not very accurate except at extremely close range. He smiled at her.

"Sit down," she said again. Her voice shook a little. "What is the matter with you? Don't you know what Slago is like? Would you leave your girl to him?"

"I have a feeling it's too late for Angelina already."

"No, Slago didn't. . . ." She paused as Durell moved toward her. She smiled. "You're mistaken, too. You think I won't shoot here. But I can. You're a thief, an intruder—"

He jumped for the gun. The blast was like a burst of thunder in the high, echoing room, and then he drove her hand aside with a sweep of his arm and brought his arm back up again to crash against her body and slam her backward. She fired again, and he saw she wanted to kill him. The first bullet had smashed into the wall. The second slammed into the ceiling. Dust drifted down on them. He heard someone shouting, muffled by the walls, and then he got the gun away from her and threw her to one side and kicked the weapon in the other direction. The blonde fell against the wall, grabbing at the telephone table for support, and knocked it over. She was breathing hard. Her eyes were furious, hating him.

"All I want is in," he said. "I intend to move in."

"Into your grave," she whispered. "Into a deep, dark hole."

"I want a part of it. The girl and I came all the way up here to join you. You could use me. You need me. Remember that. I'll give you a little time to think it over."

"We'll kill her," Jessie breathed.

"No, you won't. Remember that, too. You won't kill her."

Somebody pounded on the door, and then a key rattled, and he knew Erich Corbin had returned. This wasn't the time to talk business. He was thinking of Angelina and how to get her away from them. He knew the blonde was smart. He could see she was smart by the way she considered him now. Her anger was gone; she was weighing him, thinking how he might be useful. He saw her face relax.

"I'm leaving," he said. "I don't want to waste time talking to your husband. You're the one who runs things, so think it over. You can use a man like me. And I can use you. A strictly business proposition. What about using me?"

"Just who are you?" she whispered.

"A guy who wants a cut of the pie."

"Will you be back? I want to think—"

"I'll be back."

He turned to the windows on the fire escape and got one open just as Erich Corbin called excitedly from the foyer. He heard Jessie answer him, running down the ornate hallway, her heels clicking. He had given her something to consider. Maybe it wouldn't work out too badly, after all. . . .

He got out onto the fire escape. The courtyard below was dark, and it had stopped raining. Lights bloomed in the flat above, and a woman's voice rattled excitedly about hearing two shots. From inside the Corbin apartment he still heard Erich's voice, too. Durell turned and raced down the steel steps into the darkness of the courtyard. He ran toward the gate in the back fence and unlocked it and got out. He looked up before he closed the gate and saw Erich Corbin leaning from the window above, trying to get a look at him. Then he turned and started down the alley.

But he didn't get very far.

A shadow moved with a soft, sliding step behind him and a voice said, "All right, you. Stop trying to run, Lift 'em."

He reacted instinctively, turning with his weight on his right foot, swinging. He saw the blue uniform and the faint gleam of the badge a second too late. It was the cop on the beat. He had been alerted by Jessie's two wild shots. Durell couldn't check his swing. It was no good, anyway. The cop was young and enthusiastic. His gun crashed down at Durell and he stepped back in the alley out of reach of Durell's hands and then he hit Durell again, taking advantage of his surprise.

Durell wanted only to get away. He didn't want to fight the cop or hurt him. He tried to break free, but the cop was too good. He hit Durell once more and then there was the sound of a whistle at the open end of the alley and another cop came charging in and Durell finally began to fight him off in earnest. But it was too late by then.

He was aware only of ironic dismay as he sank back against the courtyard fence and let the young cop jab his gun savagely into his belly.

Chapter Fifteen

FROM an angle of his cell door in the precinct station, Durell could see an electric clock on the corridor wall. It was three minutes after ten. He had been booked and fingerprinted and thrown in here and nothing had happened since. He wondered if the cops would pull in the Corbins. He hoped not. It had gone worse than he had expected. He didn't want the police questioning the Corbins, or interfering with them. And he knew that time was precious, and every moment that passed put him farther behind in the race; but there was nothing he could do about it. The identification he had given to the police told them nothing about his real occupation. He couldn't tell the police anything. Wittington had ordered him not to, and MacCreedy and the FBI had to be kept out of it for now.

He went back to the cot in his cell and sat down and lit a cigarette. He thought of Angelina and then he put the thought of her out of his mind, because he couldn't think straight when he considered what might be happening to her at this very moment. The cell smelled of the heat of the past day, of urine and sweat and human misery.

His head ached where the cop had slugged him, and an intern had come in briefly and swabbed at the cut and taped some plaster over it and had gone away again. Before being brought to the cell, Durell had asked to be allowed to make one phone call. It had been granted grudgingly. The desk sergeant had lifted surprised eyes when he had called Washington, laying money on the desk for the toll charges. He had called the number of McGuire, Sloan & Levy in Washington. It was after eight o'clock by then, but an answering service had replied, much to his relief, and he had asked for Mr. Wittington. Wittington was not available. The answering service would try to trace him. They would call back when he was located.

111

Durell had to be satisfied with that. There was nothing else he could do. Wittington had tied his hands with the orders he had given him, and just calling him had been a severe breach of security, but that couldn't be helped. He had to get out of here. He couldn't spend any more time in this place. But he had already been here over two hours.

He finished the cigarette and got up to look at the clock again. 10:15. He heard voices from down the corridor, two men arguing in low tones, and he smelled cigar smoke through the other smells of the precinct station. Impatience seethed in him. He couldn't help thinking about Angelina, and he could only hope that his parting words to Jessie Corbin had given her reason to pause. One thing he was sure about was that he was too late to keep them under surveillance here in New York. They were certain to be gone by now, unless the police had detained them, too, over the shooting. But apparently, since there had been no sign of them here, they had managed to talk their way out of any implication in the disturbance.

Finally footsteps came down the corridor and a detective whom Durell hadn't seen before signaled to the turnkey to open the cell door.

"All right, chum, come out of there."

Durell stepped out. The detective had keen eyes that raked his face and clothing with open curiosity. "Come on, follow me . . . It's all right, Dave."

Durell walked down the hall to a small room in front of the desk sergeant's office. The detective sat down behind a plain oak table and shoved an envelope toward him. "Here are your things, including the gun."

"Thanks," Durell said.

"Mind answering one question?"

"That depends," Durell said.

"Who are you?"

"I can't tell you any more than I've told the sergeant."

The detective nodded. "I've got a lot on my back, thanks to you. A ton of bricks fell on me because of your call to Washington. You bastards can really free-wheel around when you want to. I wouldn't mind being in your shoes."

"I don't think you'd like it," Durell said.

The detective considered this and nodded again. "No,

maybe I wouldn't. I've got a wife and four kids. No, I guess I wouldn't."

"Can I go now?"

"Sure, go ahead. Good luck."

Durell went out without learning the detective's name.

THE rain earlier that evening hadn't helped to clear up the muggy atmosphere over New York, but the air outside felt comparatively fresh and clean after his two hours in the precinct station. Durell walked west toward Lexington and when he found a drugstore he sorted out his change and telephoned Washington again. He figured Wittington would be waiting to hear from him.

Daniel Kincaid answered the phone when he got through.

"It's a kick in the teeth," Durell said. "They got away from me and they've got the girl, Angelina Greene, too."

"I warned you about that girl—" Kincaid began angrily.

"Shut up," Durell said. His voice was suddenly ferocious. "If anybody's got a beef, it's me. You tie my hands and blindfold me and then send me out to do a decent job; and when something goes wrong, you blow your stack and take your goddam good time giving me a hand. Go ask your prediction machine what the chances of survival are under the conditions you sent me out on, in this job."

"Listen, don't tell me—"

Durell blew air out through his nostrils. He knew his anger sprang from his fears for Angelina and his dismay at the way it had all gone wrong. He forced his voice down to a more moderate level. "Kincaid, I know where they've gone. I'm going to check their apartment and the hotel where the two men stayed, but I'm sure they've already left. I think they're heading for Pennsylvania, for a town named Groversville."

"Never heard of it. Why are they going there?"

"Just listen," Durell said. "I'm going after them. They've got some blueprints of a pretty complex installation there. It's got an architect's name on it—Carl Amberley. Look it up. Put it through your machine, if you have to. Find out who Amberley is and where the blueprints came from. That's their objective, whatever it is. And whatever it is, it's big."

113

Kincaid sounded more moderate now, too. "All right, Durell. Sorry I blew my cork. You weren't supposed to contact us, you know, except in an absolute emergency."

"It is an emergency."

"Take it easy," Kincaid said. "And look, I think you'd better stay where you are in New York, where we can reach you. Don't try to trail them alone. I'll find out about this Amberley and I'll let you know. Maybe that will be the key to this whole business, understand?"

"I'm going after them," Durell insisted. "I'm not staying in town. They've got Angelina, I told you."

"You know better than to risk anything for that girl."

"I've got to risk it."

"Forget about her, do you understand?"

There were white lines at the corners of Durell's mouth. "I'll call you from Groversville when I get there," he said, and hung up.

I T WAS perhaps the biggest risk he had taken yet. Maybe Groversville had nothing to do with the objective Jessie Corbin had set for herself. Maybe he was heading in a totally wrong direction, set to wind up with a big fat zero for his score. But it was the only direction open to him, he decided, when he returned to the house in the East Seventies and made his way back to the Corbin apartment. His lock picks got him inside again. They were gone with the clothing, suitcases, and the rolls of blueprints he had left on the bed. He had expected nothing else, and it gave him a little hope.

He retrieved his rented car from where he had parked it in the neighborhood and drove downtown, parked it again in a nearby garage, and walked to Mark Fleming's hotel. Slago and Fleming were gone, too. They had not checked out officially, and the desk clerk thought they were still in residence. Durell would have liked to get into the room to see if Angelina had left any trace there, but he had no authority to demand a pass key and he didn't want to spend time getting such authority from anyone in New York who might be able to help.

He asked the clerk, "How long ago did Mr. Fleming leave?"

The clerk was thin and dapper and supercilious. He kept looking at the thin strip of surgical tape on Durell's forehead. "About an hour ago, I guess. I really didn't pay much attention."

"Was he alone?"

"No. His associate was with him."

"No one else?"

"No."

Durell put a twenty-dollar bill on the registration pad. "Think again. Didn't they have a girl with them? A tall brunette, who seemed to be a little sick?"

"Drunk, you mean," the clerk said.

"All right, drunk."

"Yes, now that I recall, she was with them."

So Angelina was alive when they checked out. Durell felt better about it. A little better, not much.

"It happens all the time in a joint like this," the clerk said. "Now, when I was manager at the Wharton-Savoy, we wouldn't have permitted anything like that to go on in the premises."

Durell thanked him and left, retrieved his car after paying an exorbitant fee for twenty minutes' parking. He hadn't eaten since lunch in Washington, but there was no time. He started driving, picking up a road map at the first service station he came to, and when he had located Groversville in the north central section of Pennsylvania, he worked out the fastest and straightest route he could find and headed that way.

It was a long, hard drive. He took Route 6, heading west, and he kept his speed just a little above the limit, not wanting the delay of being stopped for a traffic violation, although every instinct in him shouted for him to tramp on the gas pedal and make faster time. He had seen the green Buick station wagon the Corbins were using now, when he had watched their house from the room across the street. He knew that they would be equally anxious to avoid being stopped by a traffic cruiser, but even if they were driving no faster than he, they still had almost two hours on him.

And there was no telling what had happened by now.

By midnight he was through Port Jervis and into the Poconos. There was no sign of the Buick ahead. He stopped at a roadside diner and ate roast beef and drank three cups of coffee, and by four o'clock in the morning he reached the outskirts of Groversville.

THERE was little to see of the town at this dark hour. It was cooler here, on the edge of a wilderness of high, rounded mountains covered with dense woods, with here and there the probing scar of an abandoned or worked-out coal mine. There was a colliery outside of town, gaunt and stained and apparently closed years ago when the anthracite veins gave out; and as he drove through the dark, silent main street of the town Durell decided that the economy had shifted from the coal industry to catering to vacationers who sought the mountains for the summer. There was a high proportion of guest houses with small electric signs on the lawns, and a reasonably new motel on the western outskirts of town. He looked at the motel's parking lot carefully, but the green Buick wasn't there, and he faced the hopelessness of searching for it before daylight.

He was in luck when he woke up the proprietor and asked for a room. There was one vacancy. Durell bought a tooth brush and a razor and paid double the normal fee to soothe the man's trouble before going to the room assigned to him.

The moment he stepped inside, he felt as if he were back in the precinct cell again. He wanted to get out of there at once, to keep driving somewhere, anywhere, and go on looking for the Corbins and Angelina. He forced himself to close the door and turn the latch behind him, and he drew a deep breath to steady himself. For hours, while driving, he had refused to let himself think too much about Angelina; he couldn't let go now. He knew what the penalty might be if he acted on impulse, without an objective plan, and thinking of this made him calmer. He lit a cigarette and went into the bathroom and shaved carefully. Then he took a shower, first very hot, then ending it with a needle spray of cold water. It made him feel better. He still had a couple of hours till daylight, and then a couple more before the town woke up and he could ask some questions.

He was drying himself after the shower when there came a quick, quiet knock on the door, and when he wrapped a towel around himself and went to open it, he saw the thin proprietor who had rented him the room.

"Saw your light still on and figured you might need something to help you rest," the man said.

"Like what?"

"Maybe a little bourbon? This town is pretty dry. Good liquor is hard to get. You interested?"

"Some bourbon would be fine."

"Got it right here. Fifteen bucks."

Durell looked at the man and saw nothing but bland thievery on his face, so he went back into the room and got his wallet and paid for the bottle. "I need some information," he said. "Will you join me?"

"Thanks. I can't sleep, either. My wife snores."

Durell laughed and got the two tumblers from the bathroom and filled each half full and handed one to the proprietor. The man bobbed his narrow head in thanks and drank thirstily. Durell watched him for a moment before taking a drink himself.

The man said: "I could let you have some shirts and a change of underwear. I notice you've got no luggage."

"I had to travel unexpectedly," Durell said.

"Pushing on in the morning?"

"That depends. I have some business in your town."

"Only business here is tourist business, these days."

"Mine is something else. I'm looking for Carl Amberley."

"Oh, him." Durell waited. "He's got a summer place up here," the proprietor said.

"Is he in town now?"

"Could be."

"And what's his business?"

"I thought you might know," the man said cagily. "You're the one wants to deal with him."

"Is it such a big secret?"

"Hell, no. He's an architect. Big shot, from New York. Quiet enough fellow, though. Got something wrong with him. Bad heart, or something, ready to give out. Spends all summer here. No visitors."

DURELL pressed him for directions to get to Amberley's summer lodge on Kittitimi Mountain, and then he said: "One more thing. Is there a real estate agent in town named George Johnston?"

"Sure. Old George is right on Main Street. Specializes in summer rentals. You can't miss it. He opens at nine sharp. You want me to bring you some fresh shirts?"

"Not if they're more than ten bucks each."

"Make it eight."

"All right. In the morning."

"Uh . . . you want the rest of this bottle?"

"Help yourself," Durell said.

When the proprietor had gone, Durell turned off the lights and stretched out on the bed and tried to sleep.

117

He wondered if he had made a mistake, coming here. Maybe the blueprints didn't mean anything. Maybe he had jumped to conclusions about them, and they didn't represent Corbin's target. Or maybe they had changed their plans since Angelina had interfered and he himself had appeared in the picture. Jessie Corbin knew he had seen the blueprints. It might frighten her off, or cause her to postpone her plans. On the other hand, by his very appearance, he might have pushed a panic button for them and made them start running. Wherever they went, they would take Angelina, if she were still alive—or even if she were dead. They couldn't leave her body for him to find too quickly.

If this was the target area, and if he could trace them in the locality tomorrow, then he would know that he and Angelina had not alarmed them too much. They had been sure of their anonymity in New York; the police had no clue to their identity. If he had sold Jessie Corbin with his argument that he wanted a cut of their operation, then they would go ahead—watching for him, of course, wary of his being on their trail, but not worried enough to conceal or postpone their plans.

He closed his eyes upon a swimming darkness and saw Angelina. He saw her as she had been long ago, in the bayous, as wild and passionate as the land itself, giving herself without restraint or demands. She was a confident, beautiful, intelligent woman. She loved him. She had almost wrecked everything, but he felt no anger or bitterness toward her. He understood her and felt an affinity toward her because she had shared all the things that had made him what he was now. Whatever happened, he had to do what he could for her.

When he fell asleep, it was with the suddenness of a dark curtain falling over the turmoil in his mind.

Chapter Sixteen

AT SEVEN o'clock Durell was up and showered. He found two new shirts on the doorsteps of his motel room and he used one, grateful for its freshness. He

118

found a diner not far down the road where he ate with a surprising appetite and listened to the sleepy conversation of the short-order man whose chief complaint was that the tourists here usually camped out and bought their own food supplies.

The town itself showed signs of a severe economic depression not too many years in the past; a great many business places were vacant, the colliery was a lifeless area, and the coal company town on the southern fringes was a gray tumble of ruins under the bright blue sky. On the other hand, as he had noted last night, a thriving tourist industry had sprung up; and he could appreciate why. The air was crisp and cool, the sun was warm, and the mountains to the north looked virginal and inviting.

The real estate office of George Johnston was still closed, and he remembered it would not open until nine. He decided to look up Carl Amberley first, and chose a tarred road that went north out of town into the foothills ahead. For two miles he could still see the heaps of slag and waste in the valleys, and then these gradually fell away and the road turned to gravel and climbed sharply into cool pine woods. Here and there were smaller private roads, with names painted on rustic signs; and occasionally he glimpsed a summer cottage tucked away near a limpid blue lake. Following the motel proprietor's instructions, he turned right after crossing a rough wooden bridge over a mountain stream and saw the sign that read *C. Amberley*. In a moment more the house came into view.

It was modern, combining native granite with rough-hewn vertical planking, and a vast window wall caught the brightness of the sun as it lifted over the wooded mountains to the east. The road became crushed stone that circled around a small terraced lawn overlooking a private lake. When Durell parked in front of the yellow-gold doorway, he heard the increasing chorus of birds and small animal life in the woodlands.

No one was in sight, and there was no sign that anyone was awake yet, but a black Jaguar sedan was parked in the shelter of a carport.

Then, as Durell got out of his rented car, he saw someone pulling aside the heavy draperies behind the window wall. He walked up to the door along a pathway lined with oddly distorted pieces of sculpture; he couldn't find a bell, so he knocked, and waited.

While he waited he saw about thirty Canadian geese feeding in the reeds along the lake shore; a tanager flashed red in the pine woods nearby, and a squirrel came along the path behind him and sat up, waiting expectantly. There was not another house in view.

When the door opened, a plump little woman with gray hair and apple-red cheeks stood there in a brocaded housecoat. Her smile was warm and friendly. "Yes?"

"Mrs. Amberley?" When she nodded, Durell said: "I'm sorry to intrude at this hour, but it's imperative that I talk to your husband without delay."

"Oh, but I couldn't possibly—"

"It's very urgent, Mrs. Amberley."

"It always is, isn't it? You government people are always doing something urgent. I'm sorry Carl ever undertook to work for you."

"What makes you think I'm from the government, Mrs. Amberley?"

She looked puzzled. "Well, aren't you?"

"As a matter of fact, yes. But I didn't realize your husband had been disturbed so much lately."

"It hasn't been so bad, actually. Not since that darned old project was finished. You're the first in several months." She smiled suddenly and held the door open. "Come in. I expect you could use a cup of coffee."

Durell followed her into a stone-floored foyer with vines growing up the granite walls, then into the living room, which had a view of the lake. There was a huge fireplace with a copper hood suspended over it, bucket chairs of wrought iron and canvas, more growing vines, and a superb view of Kittitimi Mountain. Mrs. Amberley looked worried again.

"Carl needs his rest so much. It's his heart, you know. He had a really severe attack just six weeks ago, and he's supposed to stay in bed until noon."

"I won't trouble him for long," Durell said. "I want just to talk to him for a few minutes—he doesn't have to get out of bed."

"I'll see if he's awake."

WHEN she had gone, Durell started to light a cigarette, then saw there were no ashtrays in the big, sunlit room, and he put the cigarette away. He waited, watching the Canadian geese by the shore of the lake. The rising sun made a dazzling glare over the dark shoulder of the mountain, and the surface of the lake was momentarily ruffled by a small wind that broke up the colors in it into rippling fragments. He turned as he heard the woman's footsteps hurrying back. She came into the room alone. Her face was pale; her eyes were alarmed.

"He's not there! He's gone! We sleep in separate rooms, you see—he rests better that way. And his bed is empty. And the window is open." She put a hand to her mouth. "I don't know what it means."

"Could he have gone out for a walk?"

"Oh, no, he never does that. Not since his last attack." Her voice broke suddenly. "Why are you here? What kind of trouble—"

He made his voice quiet and soothing. "There is no trouble, Mrs. Amberley. Please don't get upset. May I see your husband's bedroom?"

She nodded quickly and led him down a short hall to the bedroom wing of the house. The door was open, and he followed her into a vast, quiet room with a beamed ceiling and more cut granite in the walls and a terra cotta floor. There was a large bed with an elaborate headboard opposite the window wall. There were two glass doors in the wall to match the window units, and one of them stood open onto a small terrace backed by a dry stone wall where wild morning glories grew. The sheets and blanket on the bed had been rumpled, but there was no real sign of any disturbance. Mrs. Amberley murmured something and Durell went past her to step outside. The wrought-iron table and chairs were wet with dew, and a path led up fieldstone steps into the woods that encroached against the back of the house. He thought he heard a waterfall tinkling quietly somewhere in the woods.

Mrs. Amberley joined him outside. "Something is wrong. I can feel it. Carl would never do this. He has always remained in bed until noon, just as the doctor said he should."

"What was the government project he worked on, Mrs. Amberley?"

Her eyes widened. "Well, gracious, don't you know? I'm sure I haven't the faintest idea."

"Wasn't it in this vicinity?"

"I suppose so, but Carl couldn't tell me anything about it." She regarded him with sudden suspicion. "Why should you ask me that? You said you were from the government. Aren't you familiar with the Kittitimi Project?"

"Not in any detail."

She backed a step away from him. "I'm going to call the police. No, the FBI. Carl—"

He couldn't tell her not to do it. He saw in this a repetitive pattern that had followed him since his trip to Louisiana. He was too late again. Corbin had moved swiftly and accurately, beating him to the objective. He had no doubt that the Corbins had Amberley now. But this settled one thing. He had come to the right place. He hadn't made a mistake about that.

Mrs. Amberley hurried ahead into the house again; her breathing was quick and frightened. Durell followed her, but when she started to lift the telephone, he put his hand on it. "Let me call Washington first, please."

She looked at him in growing terror. "Will you notify the police?"

"I'll get instructions on it, Mrs. Amberley. Perhaps your husband is simply outside. Why don't you call to him or walk around a bit to see if he isn't sitting down somewhere?"

She bit her lip. "He isn't out there, I'm sure. But I understand, I think. I'll go look."

Durell called Wittington's number as she hurried away. This time Wittington himself came on promptly, his dry voice sharp with recrimination. "What do you think you're up to?"

"Did Kincaid check the names I gave him last night?"

"Where are you, Durell?"

"Groversville. Our party is here."

"Are you sure of that?"

"They've got Carl Amberley. Have you checked him yet?"

"They've got—"

"He's missing. I'm at his house now."

There was a brief silence. Durell stared at an abstract painting on the wall as Wittington said: "You don't know who he is?"

"Look, stop horsing around. You may be the boss, but I'm here on the spot. What kind of project did he design around here?"

"We don't know yet. We're up against a blank wall."

"Well, break it down," Durell said. "This is urgent."

122

"It must be. There's an installation of some kind there, but nobody at the Pentagon knows about it or is willing to talk about it. Haven't you run into anything specific yet?"

"No. There's no sign of anything around."

"I'll have to go to the White House, then," Wittington said. "You understand? Somebody pays for this. All this damned useless secrecy and classification and red tape can go too far. I'll ask the top. I'll put a crash priority on getting the information for you."

"MacCreedy may work into this. Mrs. Amberley is going to call the FBI," Durell said. "And I can't stop her."

"It may take some time before it reaches MacCreedy."

"Too much time."

"Do you need help?"

"I don't know," Durell said. "I don't know what to look for."

"What's the number there? I'll call you back."

"I won't be here. I'll call you," Durell said, and hung up.

Mrs. Amberley came back into the house. One glance at her stricken face told Durell that her brief search had been unsuccessful. He handed the phone to her silently and told her he would drive down the road a bit and that he would call her to find out if her husband had turned up. He didn't expect anything from that, but talking to her as if her husband were not in serious danger helped her nerves somewhat.

I T WAS after nine when he returned to Groversville. The realty office of George Johnston was open. Durell parked on Main Street and watched some girls in Bermuda shorts cycling through the traffic. Then he pushed the door open to Johnston's office and went in.

George Johnston was easy to talk to. He was a plump, voluble man who offered information with easy gratuity. When Durell described the Corbins, he nodded eagerly and went to his files.

"Oh, yes, I rented them Happy Acres Lodge on Kittitimi."

"Happy Acres," Durell said.

"Lovely place. Very comfortable."

"And they have privacy, I'm sure," Durell said.

"Oh, yes. Really remote."

"Are they here now?"

"I couldn't say. I haven't seen them."

Durell asked for information on the roads to the lodge and Johnston described the back roads he had to take. "Perhaps I could interest you in a rental for the rest of the summer? Near your friends? Rates are down now—it's so close to Labor Day—but it's really the best part of the season up here."

"I'll drop back after I've seen the Corbins," Durell said.

"Do that. We'll be happy to be of service."

Durell went to the street door, and then walked back again. Johnston would know what was happening to real estate properties in the area, he decided. "One more thing. Where is the big government project around here?"

Mr. Johnston looked totally blank and smiled uncertainly. "Government project? There isn't any."

"Well, hasn't there been a big construction deal around?"

"Oh, you must mean Number Four. The Blue Spot Colliery. That old anthracite mine they thought they could reopen last year."

"Yes, that must be the one," Durell said.

"You're late, if you're selling anything. You can't even go there now—it's all private property. They bought up half the mountain." Johnston looked resentful of this. "Big disappointment to everybody in town. The mines have been worked out since '52, and everybody had high hopes they'd be revived when Blue Spot began hauling in all those trainloads of equipment. But nothing came of it. A lot of fuss and money spent, and the vein didn't last at all. I understand Blue Spot went completely under in the gamble."

"I'd like to visit the place, anyway. Is it possible?"

"Well, they put up fences and all, and posted the place against hunters and trespassers. Might've thought they were mining gold, folks said. But the property goes for miles, I guess. Half the mountain, like I said. I wouldn't want to suggest that you do anything illegal, like trespassing—"

"Doesn't Blue Spot have an office in town where I could get permission to see the site?"

"Not around here, that's for sure. Maybe in New York."

124

"I see. Well, thanks."

"Not at all. If you're interested in a summer rental—"

"I'll be back," Durell said.

He had a cup of coffee in a restaurant next door and then walked over to the Town Hall and consulted the topographical maps of the county on the walls, and then asked for the township plots that included Kittitimi Mountain. He spent over half an hour with the maps, and when he came out, he had the geography of the area well fixed in his mind. He called Mrs. Amberley, and the woman said there was no trace of her husband anywhere. The local sheriff was sending up a deputy to investigate. She was worried lest her husband had gotten up for a walk in the night, and perhaps had fallen into the lake and drowned. Durell didn't tell her that her husband might have preferred that sort of an end to the one waiting for him at Slago's hands.

He considered calling Washington again, but the circuits were busy, and he no longer could resist the pressure of impatience and worry that gnawed at him. He returned to his car and drove as fast as he could toward the looming mountain in the north.

Chapter Seventeen

A NGELINA watched the sunlight go brighter and stronger as the sun came up over the high shoulders of the mountain. She watched the strengthening light with eyes that were dull and blank. She had not closed them all night, but she did not feel tired. She no longer felt any pain. She didn't feel anything, and somewhere deep in the back of her shocked mind she knew she wanted to keep it that quiet nothingness. She resented the daylight that gradually intruded through the cracks in the shutters locked across the window. It brought her back to reality, and she fought against that because the reality of what had happened to her was too ugly to accept.

The woman had been kind enough, in an impersonal way. Jessie, they called her. She was the older man's

125

wife. She had insisted they stop the station wagon at one point during the long ride that night and she bought some bandages and antiseptic stuff at an all-night drugstore and she had taken care of the things Slago had done with his knife.

No, don't think about that, she told herself.

She stirred and hugged herself and shivered in the cool morning air. She didn't know where she was, and she didn't care. Nothing mattered any more, after what Slago had done. She looked down at her arms folded around her middle, and she was surprised to find herself wearing a gray flannel dress. The blonde woman must have given it to her. Her own clothes had been worse than useless. For a moment, Angelina almost unzipped the dress to look down at the body she had been so proud of. But she couldn't look at herself. She never wanted to see herself again. Nobody would ever look at her disrobed without shuddering, she thought. And the feeling she had for Sam was over and finished, done with forever. It seemed only a short time ago when she had been planning to offer herself in simple, uncomplicated pleasure she could give him, and proud of what she could offer. No more. Never again. No one would want her like this, ever again.

She told herself not to think about that, or about the dull pain that Jessie's aspirins had failed to kill. Think about Peche Rouge, she told herself. About the past, where things were safe and sure and settled. She looked around the room.

Sunlight came through the cracks in the shutters and placed bright yellow bars of gold on a hooked rug spread over the pine floor. The walls were half logs, chinked with plaster, but the windows were modern steel casements. She looked up slowly at the raftered ceiling. There were wasp nests up there, but the morning was too chilly for them to be active. A feeling of disuse and mildew clung to the furnishings and touched the room with a damp finger. The bed was old, with brass pipe framing. A battered armchair, a Grand Rapids dresser with the veneer curling at the edges, and the wooden chair she sat in completed the inventory. She was sorry there was nothing else to look at. Looking around kept her from thinking about Slago.

The place was quiet. They had all gone out and then two of them had come back, the sounds of their feet angry on the floor outside. She could not remember what the rest of the house looked liked when they had arrived. She tried, but nothing came back to her. She had shrunk away into some deep, dark place inside herself when they had come back at dawn. She had thought Slago would come in here again. But the door had remained closed and nobody had even bothered to look in at her. She had smelled bacon and eggs and coffee and for a little while she had been hungry; but nobody fed her, and now she wasn't hungry any more.

When she looked at the floor again, she saw that the sunlight had moved quite a few inches across the hooked rug. She sighed and touched her body where the bandages were. The house was so quiet. Where had they gone? Why had they left her alone like this? She was reluctant to get up, because as long as she sat unmoving and unnoticed, she felt safer, somehow. But she got to her feet and looked at the door. It was just a simple batten door with an old-fashioned wrought-iron thumb latch. Was it locked? She was afraid to find out. She was afraid somebody was out there.

Where would she go, even if she got out?

She stood still for a time, standing in the shapeless gray dress that covered her. She heard a bird singing. She heard the sound of running water tumbling over stones. She heard an airplane high in the invisible sky. She heard someone groan in the next room.

Then there was silence again. And another groan.

She drew back from the door. She could not understand it. She thought it was a trap. She trusted nothing and nobody. Someone walked with a slow, painful step across the floor beyond the door. Angelina moved toward the panel again.

"Hello?"

She was startled by the sound of her own voice.

"Hello?" she called again.

The footsteps halted. There was quiet; the birds sang; the water ran over the rocks outside. Then there came a slow fumbling as someone slid a bolt aside on the door of her room. She shrank back again.

"No, don't . . ."

A MAN stood there, looking at her. She hadn't seen this one before. He looked ill, a man with white hair and deep lines of suffering in his handsome face. He wore pajamas, but Angelina did not think this was particularly singular. His feet were bare and bloody, there were livid bruises on his face, and he held one arm as if it had been broken. He breathed queerly, as if every breath hurt him and he wished he could stop breathing, but he couldn't.

"My God, what have they done to *you?*" the man whispered.

"Who are you?"

"Amberley. Carl Amberley. They kidnaped me early this morning. What did they do to you?"

"I don't know. I don't want to think about it."

"How long have you been here?"

"I don't know."

"Well, don't you want to get away?"

She looked blank. She had buried the thought and hope of escape so deep in her mind that it was difficult to bring it back to the surface and look at it again.

"Are you all right?" the man asked gently.

"Yes. No. I don't know. They did things— Why aren't they here?"

"They've all gone, and we're locked in." His voice was bitter, defeated. "They made me tell. I was weak. I have a very bad heart, young lady, and I thought they were going to kill me. I suppose the more intimate one becomes with death, the greater the cowardice for some of us. I thought they were going to kill me, and when that man with the knife—"

"Don't," she said quickly. She shuddered. "Don't mention him."

"But they got the information from me—"

"You couldn't help it. Please, sit down. You can't help me, either. You don't look well at all."

"They're all gone, and I've got to get out of here. But I don't seem to have the strength I need."

She looked at him and suddenly realized that for the last moment or two she had forgotten to think about herself. "Sit down," she said. "I'll look around. Don't you have any shoes?"

"They took me out of my bed."

"Maybe I can find you some."

"What about you?" You're barefooted, too. And in these mountains—"

"Do you know where we are?" she asked.

"Of course. Don't you?"

"They took me from New York. Never mind; just sit down." Her voice had tightened. She saw he was having trouble breathing. "Please, sit down. I'll be right back." She even managed to smile. "And thanks for letting me out of my cage."

He started to ask her why she was a prisoner, too, but she didn't wait around to reply. The room she was in served as a living room, typically rustic for a mountain lodge, with wide-pegged floors, a fieldstone fireplace with a mounted deer's head over it, and pegs in the wall alongside where rifles had been kept. Somebody had thoughtfully removed the weapons. She wondered if they had been simply put out of sight, but she gave up hope for that sort of luck. There were two windows, both barred and shuttered from the outside. She tried the heavy plank door. It was also barred from the outside. Turning, she moved into a hallway that opened into a kitchen, with two bedrooms on either hand. None of the beds had been slept in. There was a back door opening onto a porch, but this was locked and the key was not in sight, and the glass panes were too small to break and crawl through. Still, she was not discouraged. She did not allow herself to think more than a step or two ahead. She was simply grateful for the moment that the Corbins and Slago and Fleming were not around.

There was a pot of coffee on the kerosene stove and she found wooden matches in the cupboard and lit the burner under the pot and returned to the living room. Amberley was sitting in a maple rocker, bent forward a little. His arm that looked broken was held at an awkward angle. She thought there were tears on his face, but she looked away from them.

"Are you all right?"

"I don't think—not really, no," Amberley whispered.

"I'll see if I can find some shoes."

"Can we get out of here?"

"I think so."

"The sooner the better, Miss—"

"Greene. Angelina Greene."

"What did they do to you?"

"Enough," she said.

She found a pair of leather moccasins in a suitcase in one of the bedrooms, and she found slippers for herself in Jessie Corbin's. The slippers were tight, but they were better than nothing. She went back to the living room again. Amberley had not moved. She knelt before him and helped him on with the moccasins.

"Do they fit all right?" she asked him.

"Yes. Fine."

"Let's see if we can get out, then."

"Do you know where to go?" he asked. "Do you have any friends around here?"

"No, but don't worry about me. You have to get to the police. You know more about all this than I do. I stumbled into it without knowing what it all meant. You're the one to tell it to the police. But first you need some coffee."

S HE went back to the kitchen. She was worried about the gray look on Amberley's face, and the way he walked, with pain and hesitation. He could not go far, she knew. But every step away from this place would be a help. She couldn't think beyond that.

She gave him a cup of coffee, and while he sipped it, she broke one of the panes of glass in the kitchen door with the heel of her borrowed slipper and reached out and felt in the lock outside to see if the key had been left there. Her groping fingers found nothing. She stood back, frustrated. Through the broken glass, she could see the woods, the side of the silent mountain, the blue of the free sky.

"It's a simple lock," Amberley said. "Let me try."

The hot coffee had helped him. He found a nut pick in the kitchen drawers and he thrust it into the lock and tinkered with it. Angelina stood by and felt despair return like a fog rolling over her mind. Why was she running away? There was no place to go. No place she could hide from herself. She touched the rough bandages on her wounds. It was as if Slago's knife had cut something out of her that couldn't be replaced.

"Here we are," Amberley said, at last.

The door swung open. He breathed heavily again. The air beyond the open door felt crisp and cool. They walked out together.

The lawn around the house was rough and shaggy. Amberley walked uncertainly. A dim trail led off into the pines in front of the house, and without a word, they started down the long slope, moving slowly because of the man's weakness. They did not look back.

The trail led down to a small bridge that spanned a

rocky, tumbling stream. The water looked cold and inviting. Angelina longed to bathe; she felt dirty; she felt as if all the water in the world couldn't wash away the filth that grimed her. But she knew she couldn't stop. This man with her suffered every step of the way, but he was going on, and the least she could do was to go on with him.

They were on the bridge when they heard the car approaching. A trick of the terrain had kept them from hearing the motor before. Angelina saw the car almost simultaneously with the sound as it came grinding around a curve in the trail and turned to the bridge. It was the green Buick station wagon, and Slago was driving.

She reacted without thinking or weighing the cost. Escape had been a dream, anyway, a prayer and a curse. Turning, she shoved Amberley off the bridge and down the little slope into the thick brush along the banks of the stream. Almost in the same moment, she ran headlong along the trail, toward the car.

Slago saw her; he stopped before he struck her, and got out, grinning. Angelina turned, pretending to be confused, and began to run in the opposite direction. He ran after her and she looked back, as if in terror. Amberley was climbing up out of the stream, staggering into the brush. Slago had not seen him. She stumbled and fell. She heard Slago crash after her like some animal hunting her down. She tried to get up, but her dress had snagged on the brush, and it held her helplessly to the soft earth until Slago caught up with her. She turned and looked up into his pale, cruel eyes. He was laughing.

"I've been waiting to get us alone again for a long time, sweetheart," he said.

Chapter Eighteen

DURELL followed the realty agent's directions and turned off the main highway to follow a dirt road that twisted up the side of Kittitimi Mountain. It was almost ten o'clock now. He had called Washington, and Wittington had ordered him to stand by at the motel until he could get some men up there to help. Durell couldn't just sit and wait. He kept thinking of Angelina and Amberley. He told Wittington that any men he sent could follow him, and then he had taken the road to the mountain.

The sun was now well over the thrusting shoulder of the pine-clad range ahead. Far below he could see the line of the abandoned colliery rails, curving up through the silently singing valleys. He knew where he was going now. He could even guess what Corbin's objective was, although Wittington had refused to tell him.

He kept watching for the little bridge that George Johnston had told him was only a quarter of a mile from Corbin's lodge. There were no other summer cottages on this road. Now and then he glimpsed rusted wire fencing through the woods and an occasional *No Trespassing* sign. He had looked curiously that way, but there seemed to be only a wilderness on that part of the mountain.

He found Amberley just a short distance from the bridge, and he quickly stopped the car. He did not get out immediately, but put his gun in his lap and waited and listened. Amberley lay face down, sprawled on the trail where he had fallen. In his pajamas, the man was unmistakable. Durell got out and walked slowly toward him.

The man was still alive. Durell felt his pulse, saw the blue tinge of the man's cyanotic lips, the broken arm. Durell's face was blank as he looked sharply toward the wooden bridge beyond. He couldn't see the Corbin cabin, but he knew it was there. And because of the silence, he knew no one was in it now. He was still too late, just a step behind them.

"Amberley, can you hear me?" he said gently. "It's all right now. I want to help you." He paused, and then asked: "Where is the girl? Angelina Greene. Wasn't she in there with you? Wasn't she a prisoner, too?"

"Prisoner, yes . . ." Amberley whispered. He opened his eyes and looked at Durell's lean, hard face. "Who are you?"

"A friend," Durell said. "You can believe that."

"Got to—stop them—"

"Where did they go?"

"I told them—told them where to go. Couldn't help it. There's so much pain . . . Can you get me to a doctor?"

"The best thing is to lie still. Where are they?"

"The girl—let them catch her again—to give me a chance to get away. But I—I couldn't make it."

Durell had nothing to ease the man's pain. He felt impatient to go on, but Amberley had something to tell him, and he had to learn what it was. "How long have you been out here?"

"Don't know . . . blacked out when he came back."

"Who?"

"The ugly one. The girl let him grab her to give me a chance—"

"Half an hour ago?"

"Maybe."

"Longer?"

"I don't know."

"What did they get out of you? You can tell me. I'm going after them."

"Follow trail . . . past lodge. Old coal mine . . . Blue Spot shack entrance . . . Look at the rails. . . ."

Amberley lowered his head. His breathing was quick and shallow. Durell felt for his pulse again. He said: "There will be some men along, right behind me, I hope. They'll take care of you."

He didn't think Amberley could hear him any more.

HE SPENT only a few minutes in the lodge. No one was there. He went through it quickly, gun in hand, finding only silence and emptiness. There was no hint as to what had happened here.

He could take the car no farther. The road ended at the cabin, and beyond there was only a hiking trail that twisted away into the woods, climbing toward the silent green shoulder of Kittitimi Mountain. Durell wasted no more time. He started walking.

The sun was hot now. Flies buzzed persistently in the dank, green underbrush, but he paid no attention. Now and then he caught a glimpse of quiet, sunlit valleys below, with the colliery rail line lifting gradually to meet him. He wondered what Amberley had meant by telling him to look at the rails. He saw that the trail would intersect the single track, abandoned line present-

133

ly, and he walked faster. When he came to the wire barrier across the trail, he did not hesitate. It was new, like the metal warning sign against trespassers that hung from it. Somebody had cut through the wires recently and gone on. A few steps beyond he found the wire clippers in the grass. They were slightly rusted, as if they had been out in the dew all night.

In twenty minutes he came to the railroad line. The trail crossed it in a narrow, wooded gorge and then swung along beside it to follow the right-of-way. The tracks had been laid recently, but not too much traffic had gone over them. The gorge opened at the northern end onto a wide slope of the mountain's face. Durell was sweating from the long, straight upward climb, and now he paused and studied the open terrain with care.

He was almost at the abandoned mine workings. A mile away he could see the cluster of gray, weathered buildings of the colliery, a faded sign hanging from one of the sway-backed roofs. The rail line ahead divided at several switch points, became a double track and then doubled again. Sunlight glinted on the ribbons of steel, and all at once he saw what Amberley wanted him to see. If the colliery had been abandoned as long ago as the public was meant to believe, those rails would have long been rusted and overgrown with weeds. But they looked new.

He studied the slope for another long minute, looking for a sign of life and movement. There was nothing to see. The face of the mountain looked jagged, with great outcroppings of granite overhanging the wooden structures below. The wind made a steady, singing pressure in his ears. He wondered if he ought to wait here for the men Wittington was sending to help, but somewhere ahead in those deserted-looking buildings was the end of the trail he had followed—a trail marked with death and the blood of innocent men. He went on.

When he had covered half a mile diagonally across the face of the slope, he saw the green station wagon. He almost missed it because it was partly hidden behind a small shack that stood higher on the mountainside than the rest of the mine structures. And Amberley apparently had not known about the road by which the Buick had been brought all the way up through this wilderness. Either that, or Amberley had supposed that the footpath would bring him here faster and more surely. It was plain that Slago, after recapturing Angelina, had discovered Amberley's escape and driven here to find the others.

He came to another high wire fence, and this one was not cut, and he lost several precious minutes seeking a way to climb over it. A long tongue of pine woods intervened at this point between the fence and the shack, and he lost sight of the Buick for a time while he moved on and finally he came out on a crag of rock overlooking the fence and the workings below. By climbing a few feet into one of the pines, he was able to drop over the barrier. Now he saw that some kind of steady activity had been going on at the site of the mine—an activity that the public had been encouraged to forget or ignore in this remote place.

The rails had been used. And there was a flat clearing to the west of the leaning colliery towers that might have been designed as a landing area for helicopters, with yellow circles painted on the asphalt apron. One of the long open sheds nearby could have been used to shelter the machines. And Durell also saw that several of the gray mine buildings were not in as rickety shape as they had appeared.

Somebody was stationed and quartered here. There was a jeep, just visible in the shadows of a small hill of waste on the lower slope. There was even a faint plume of smoke from the chimney of one of the buildings. But no one was in sight.

If any troops were quartered here, they were deep underground, and so were the Corbins and Slago and Fleming by now.

Durell moved on down toward the station wagon.

Now he became aware of a restlessness in the atmosphere, a steady pulsing and a hum of hidden machinery and he paused in the brush above the shack to study the place in detail. The station wagon looked empty. The door to the ramshackle place was open, but he couldn't see inside.

He had the feeling of being an intruder in a place far from all the everyday realities of life. The silent, subtly shifting pressures of the mountain made his nerves tense. The humming and pulsing was louder now. He moved toward the station wagon first. It was parked in tall weeds behind the shack, but a well-trodden path led to the door of the building. When he paused by the car, he saw what looked like a shapeless gray bundle of old clothes or blankets huddled on the floor of the car. Then he saw her feet and his heart lurched suddenly.

"Angelina?" he whispered.

There was no movement and no reply. He drew a deep breath. A crow screamed loudly in the pines nearby. The air of the coal mine seemed deeper and darker.

"Angelina?"

There was a faint, tentative stirring. "Sam?"

"Come out of there," he whispered.

"You're too late."

"I need help."

"I can't help you."

He reached in and touched her gray dress and she reacted violently, covering her wounded body, shrinking from his touch. Her eyes looked at him as if he were a stranger, staring in terror and shame.

"What did they do to you?" he whispered.

"I can't tell you."

"Was it Slago?"

"Yes."

"Come on out," he said again. His voice, though soft, held harsh command. She looked blankly at him. There were scratches and dirt stains on her face, and her dark hair was a long, unkempt tangle framing the pallor of her face. "Where are they?" he asked.

"Down below."

"In the mine?"

"Whatever it is," she said.

"It isn't a mine?"

"No."

He didn't like the look in her eyes, the altered expression of her mouth. He helped her out. She was very careful to keep the dress closed at her throat. She shrank from his touch. "Don't, Sam."

"It's all over. They won't hurt you again."

"They don't have to. It's all been done. I'm so dirty, dirty . . ." Her eyes stared into terrors he did not recognize. "You'll have to forget about me, Sam."

"You're alive, aren't you?" He didn't like her obsession with what had happened. "I was afraid you wouldn't be."

"I wish I were dead."

He shook her lightly. Her flesh cringed away from his grip. "How did they go in?"

"Through there." She pointed at the shack. "I almost got away, you know. There was a man, he said his name was Amberley, or something like that, and they made him tell about it. I tried to help him get away—"

"He's all right," Durell said. "I found him."

"I'm glad. And now—you've found me. I was afraid you would."

He wasn't sure, from the way she looked at him, that she really understood what was happening. He had felt a great relief at finding her. Now he was aware of anger growing, because of what had been done to her. He didn't know the details, but he could guess. His anger shook him badly and he fought it down, knowing that this was no time to get impulsive.

"Angelina, you've got to help me, too."

"Don't touch me, please."

"Hell, I'm going to kiss you."

"No!"

He caught her to him and held her tightly when she tried to squirm away. He couldn't think of any other way to force her back to reality. "There's nothing so wrong that it can't be made right again, Angelina. Do you understand? Do you know what I'm talking about?"

"You can't imagine what he—what Slago—"

"You wanted to revenge Pete once. You wanted to kill Slago, didn't you? Then let's go after them." He saw her shudder. "You're not afraid now. Come on."

He didn't want to leave her; he wasn't sure where everyone in the Corbin group might be, and he couldn't let them get her again. He saw her staring at him with great tears rolling slowly down her bruised face. "Oh, Sam, I've spoiled it all by being such a fool . . ."

"That's over with now. Let's go."

Impatience spurred him. Every moment spent was time irretrievably lost. He couldn't be late again. He walked away from her, hoping she would follow. He was at the door of the shack before he heard her quick steps behind him. He listened for sounds from inside the building, but all he heard was the humming and the pulsing and a dim, muted hissing sound.

He turned his head and looked at Angelina. She brushed at her eyes and smiled.

"All right, Sam."

The door was partly ajar. He kicked it open all the way and went in fast.

Chapter Nineteen

THERE was an inner door, and he burst through that, too. He was not prepared for the brilliant light flooding the mine shack beyond. It came from a powerful lamp in the ceiling; there was electricity still in the mine workings, although he had not spotted any power cables. A small atomic generating plant, perhaps —but he had no time to pursue the thought.

Erich Corbin came away from the opposite wall in a frantic rush.

Durell took it all in with one glance: the false roof that was really a ventilating grate covering almost the entire top area of the shack; the opposite wall of grated ducts, sucking air inside with a force powerful enough to make him feel the heavy draft of air that blew his hair almost as if he were in a wind tunnel; the twin pressure tanks Corbin had been fiddling with, the nozzles hissing into the grated openings.

"Hold it," Durell said.

Corbin's rush could not be stopped. His rimless glasses splintered light from the glaring floodlamps overhead, and his pale eyes looked wild. Durell's hand slid out, caught the waving gun in the chemist's grip, twisted it away and down as it went off with a shattering crash. A stream of German curses came from Corbin as he tried to wrench free. Durell would not let him go.

"It's all over now. So take it easy."

"You cannot stop us!"

Durell chopped at him with a short left that caught Corbin behind the ear. Corbin reeled back, and Durell clipped him with another left, and then a right that made the man's gun fly from his fingers. Corbin fell against his tanks and began to cough and small wads of saturated cotton fell from his nostrils. Durell went past Corbin while the man was still gagging, clawing at his throat and chest where Durell had chopped at him. Durell turned the tank nozzles off with several quick twists and the hissing sounds ended. Turning he saw Angelina in the doorway.

"Pick up his gun," Durell said.

She just stood there. "They've killed two soldiers."

"Soldiers?"

"They look like soldiers. They're in army uniforms."

"Where?"

"Out behind this shack."

"All right. Pick up Corbin's gun. We have a lot to do. Can you use that Luger?"

"If I pick it up," she said carefully, "I'll kill him. Don't you know that?"

Durell scooped up Corbin's Luger and thrust it into her cold hand. "You won't do anything unless I tell you to." He looked at Corbin. The man was still coughing, half strangled from the effect of Durell's blow against his larynx. "All right, Erich, where are your friends?"

"They are too far—ahead of you."

"Where?"

"Down below."

Durell picked up the nose wads, sniffed at the astringent chemicals that saturated them, and said: "How do we get down there?"

"We?"

"You lead the way."

"But the gas—"

"I imagine these ducts will sweep it out fast enough."

He saw by the look on Corbin's face that he had guessed correctly. The man coughed again, and rubbed his throat. "You know what this place is?" he whispered.

"I can guess," Durell said grimly.

"But do you know?"

"How did you find out about it?"

"Jessie has ways of learning things." Corbin's voice was steadier, stronger. "You are a stubborn man, Mr. Durell, but there is no advantage to either of us in fighting one another. Jessie told me of your proposition. If you were clever enough to follow us here, you are clever enough to be useful. I am sure something can be arranged."

"No more deals. Show us the way down." Durell turned his head. "Angelina?"

"Yes," she said.

"Shoot him if he doesn't start at the count of five."

"I'll be glad to." She sounded all right now, in command of herself.

139

Corbin looked from Durell to the girl. His thin nose looked pinched and white. He shrugged. "As you wish. Follow me."

H E WENT outside. The colliery and dilapidated mine workings still looked abandoned and ghostly. But as they walked down the rough shale of the slope, Durell saw that most of the effect of abandonment was due to a clever job of camouflage. The buildings leaned as if they were ready to topple before the next mountain storm, but they had been designed to lean that way. The roads that looked disintegrated from a distance were actually hard-packed and firm. As far as the townspeople and any occasional trespassers were concerned, the mine was only a monument to a commercial failure. And Durell doubted that anyone was ever given a chance to determine otherwise.

Corbin led the way to another building farther down the slope that looked like a power relay station, but the cables had been removed and no outside power was wired to the mine workings. Still the humming and pulsing persisted, and when Corbin went inside, Durell saw only an expanse of dusty floor with odds and ends of rusted mine machinery heaped about. Two men in civilian clothes lay bound and gagged to one side of the threshold. Their eyes were wide and frightened.

"Which way now?" he asked Corbin.

"The elevator."

Durell saw no sign of an elevator, but Corbin crossed the wide, dusty room, moving through the dim shafts of sunlight that came through the grimed windows, and when he opened a door Durell saw instead the trim, modern interior of an elevator cage. Soft, indirect lighting shone down on the controls.

"How many men did you have to knock out?" he asked.

"Over a dozen."

"And how many below?"

"I have not been below. But any others are taken care of by the gas."

"For how long?" Durell asked.

Corbin shrugged. "I increased the intensity and concentration of the formula." He looked at his watch. "All will be quiet for another half hour."

Durell waved Angelina into the elevator. Her eyes were wide with wonder and confusion. She started to

140

speak, then bit her lip and slid past him into the gray metal cage. Corbin licked his lips nervously and said: "Look here, we can be reasonable. There is enough for all of us. We are on the point of a great success. We will share with you—"

Durell hit him, swiftly and expertly. Corbin's legs buckled and he sagged to the dusty floor. Corbin would not trouble them for at least thirty minutes or more. He left the man where he was and went into the elevator with Angelina.

She was huddled against the back wall of the cage. Durell smiled tautly and considered the controls and punched the single *Down* button. She whispered a question he did not hear, and then she repeated it. "Sam, where *are* we?"

"In a coal mine."

"It's much more than a mine."

"Yes." The elevator began to descend with only a soft whining noise from its motors. Durell closed his eyes for a moment, then looked at the girl. "Are you all right?"

"I'm frightened, I guess."

"So am I, a little," he said. "We're going to get a look at the future."

"I don't know what you mean."

"We're going to see how Atomic Man will live."

"I still don't understand you."

"Maybe I should have said the Underground Man."

"Sam, please."

His mouth was bitter. "The outfit I work for is supposed to have access to everything. There isn't one plan for our defense that is supposed to be kept from my boss. But this was. Somebody in Washington has the idea that a secret defense headquarters is too vital to be known to anyone—probably even to the general staff that's supposed to man this place in time of emergency."

"You're not making any sense."

"I'm angry, that's all."

THE elevator had been descending slowly and steadily deep into the rocky heart of Kittitimi Mountain. It gave no sign of stopping yet. Durell sighed. "The men who are supposed to calculate for and take care of every contingency that might arise in our defense plan thought

141

up this place and had it built. There was never any real resurgence of mining here. It was carried on by the government, from Washington. Probably the workers who rebuilt all this didn't have much of an idea of what they were doing, and those who did were taken care of by top security clearances."

"But what were they doing?"

"Building an underground defense headquarters. Or a tomb."

"A tomb?"

"For the Atomic Man. The Underground Man. The children who inherit the future. Living like moles, away from the sun and the fresh air. Cowering and hiding in fear of the bombs."

Angelina was pale. "I think I see—"

"Jessie Corbin found out about this place. It stands to reason it had to exist. Someone had to think of continuing the government in case Washington was wiped out. So you can call this Washington Underground."

The elevator halted and the doors opened automatically.

An army corporal sprawled on the floor just beyond the shaft. Durell sniffed cautiously at the air. The ventilating pumps had scoured the place clean of Corbin's gas in the minute it had taken to descend to this level. It smelled fresh. He waited a moment, not trusting his senses, and not trusting Corbin's words. It could have been a trap. But nothing happened. He stepped out of the elevator.

A vast corridor carved out of living rock reached away before them. Indirect tubular lighting made a bluish glow everywhere. Softly lighted signs pointed to an intersecting tunnel about a hundred feet ahead, saying, *Reception, Integration, Services*, and there were numbers and arrows as in an office building, 1001-1051, and numbers and more arrows on the opposite side. A gray metal desk with a sign saying *Stop Here to Register* was apparently the fallen army corporal's station. It was equipped with a new typewriter and a teletype machine, together with a dictaphone, a file card rack, and a BAR rifle in a niche in the wall. Durell moved to the card index rack and flipped the heavy metal leaves over. All the cards were blank, waiting to be filled.

From somewhere up ahead a bell clanged softly and the teletype machine began to clatter. Durell felt Angelina grab at his arm. She was shivering, although the air was warm and comfortable.

"Where is everybody?"

"The men stationed here are just a skeleton crew, and they were all knocked out by Corbin's gas. That doesn't stop all these machines from duplicating what's going on in Washington at this minute." He paused. "Don't talk too much. We have to find the others, and our voices may carry."

Durell's flesh crawled. There was no sound except the muted beat of the power plant far below, which he was sure now was an atomic installation; and now and then there came the muted clang of a signal bell, the rattling of a teletype machine somewhere, and the ever-present hiss and pressure of air being pumped in and out of the ducts. They passed office after office, all silent and empty, all equipped with desks, machines, chairs, maps, filing cabinets. Ghost offices waiting for a ghostly personnel who might never survive to man this place. Durell hoped they would never have occasion to run for it.

He paused at the first intersection of the main corridor. To the right was the medical department, and he walked a short distance down the tunnel, glancing into empty examination rooms with fully equipped surgical cabinets, a small pale-green surgery, and a long series of wards and private rooms, each of which was equipped to the last possible detail. His feeling of eerie chill persisted when he returned to the intersection with Angelina.

No one was in sight.

He looked at his watch. There were only twenty minutes left, if he could believe Erich's remark about the potency of the gas. In that time, Jessie and Fleming would have planned to finish their raid and be out of here and away. He had to find them. There were obviously miles of tunnels, corridors, apartments, offices and barracks in Kittitimi Mine. He had only twenty minutes —nineteen, now.

ANGELINA had walked off in the opposite direction and turned a corner of the tiled corridor opposite the medical wards. He heard her soft call of surprise and ran after her. She stood before a heavy steel door with yellow lettering painted on it. *Restricted Area. Only*

Authorized Personnel Permitted. Show Your 22 Card.

One leaf of the heavy door stood ajar. Two men in army uniforms lay sprawled on the floor, victims of Corbin's gas. Angelina was peering beyond when Durell caught up with her.

"What is it?" he whispered.

"Look at those names."

There was a long series of office doors beyond the steel portal. Painted on each was the insignia of various congressional committees. Durell walked past to another door that barred his way.

The Senate. The House of Representatives.

He looked briefly into the big chambers beyond, carved out of the solid rock, softly lighted, the chairs ranged in semicircular tiers around duplicate speakers' rostrums. He felt a dryness in the back of his throat. Everything was too empty, too obviously waiting.

Angelina whispered, "They thought of everything, down to the last—"

There came a dull thumping sound, like a muffled explosion. Durell felt the pressure wall, like a puff of warm air, strike the left side of his face. He turned instinctively in that direction. Angelina put her hand on his arm.

"Sam, what was that?"

"They're down there somewhere. Back the way we came."

He ran, his feet light and silent, from the legislative chambers to the main tunnel again. Pausing, he turned left once more, and came to a wide, steel spiral staircase that bored still lower into the bowels of the mountain. The walls here were painted a bright blue. He ran down the steps as fast as he could with silence, leaving Angelina farther and farther behind. On the lower level he paused, breathing quickly and lightly. The gun felt slippery in his hand and he dried his palm on his thigh. There was nothing to see. Ahead was a sign that read *Communications.* The doors were open. He stepped inside and saw banks of teletypewriters and a large electronic computer. Lights winked solemnly at him from the faces of the machines, and the teletypewriters occasionally belled softly and rattled, with no one to read the messages that rolled out on long strips of yellow paper. Durell paused to look at one of them. It was a routine news dispatch from Los Angeles apparently concerning the production figures of a new jet fighter. It was headed for the attention of *ComSecDef*. He frowned, wondering if another machine in Washington was repeating the identical message for the information of a congressional committee or a staff officer in the Pentagon. He saw a pattern in the installations that repeated, on each machine, the activity going on at every moment in Washington. Everything that could be duplicated in the essential functions of government had been reproduced in this hollow mountainside. In this labyrinth the government functioned on automation, kept up to date to the split second, guarded by a select skeleton crew of maintenance men who were ready at any moment to receive the fugitive officials from any wartime catastrophe that could rain paralyzing, annihilating bombs upon the nerve centers of the United States. Everything had been prepared for. The jobs of defense, rehabilitation, and restoration of normal life were waiting here.

A normal life? Durell wondered. He drew a deep breath. Here was the future, unless statesmen proved more gifted, and humanity veered from the insanity of atomic war. Here was a future that could exist only underground.

The explosion he had heard was not repeated.

He paused, trying to put himself in the place of those he hunted. What were they after? Slago and Fleming wanted money. He did not know about Jessie Corbin. Her motives were more subtle and devious. Durell looked at an electric clock on the wall of the communications room. Seventeen minutes left.

Suddenly he turned and began to run, searching for the obvious objective. Angelina hurried silently after him, Corbin's Luger gripped in her hand. When Durell came to another tunnel, he saw he was in a new restricted area devoted to cabinet officers. The names of each department of the government was painted in signs over the doorways—Commerce, Agriculture, State, Justice, Defense, Treasury.

He slammed open the last door.

He stood in a maze of offices, all softly lighted, all empty and waiting. A familiar scent touched him, pumped along on the current of air filtering through the mountain labyrinth. It was the smell of powder, the odor of an explosion. He followed it, running lightly along the corridors, and then he suddenly came upon a vast, circular room, furnished with desks, tables, tellers' cages, a vault in the rear.

It figured, Durell thought, that if they planned a complete national headquarters like this, somebody in the Treasury Department would have a hand in it, too. In the sort of national catastrophe that would require this place, there would be financial panic, a run on money, perhaps the destruction of the government mints and printing plants. There had to be a cache of currency here, hundreds of millions, planned for release and distribution among the surviving populace to restore monetary confidence. Jessie Corbin must have learned about it. She would have a lot to tell, that woman. Where she got the information, how she got it, who the traitor is. But that was how she got Slago and Fleming to do her dirty work for her, Durell thought. She promised them the biggest cache of currency in the country.

THE door to the vault was partly open. The muffled blast he had heard a few moments ago had knocked the heavy door off its hinges. The door had not been as solid or secure as any surface bank vault. Down here, there had been no need for it. Light streamed from inside the vault. Durell put out a hand and stopped Angelina. He held his gun ready. He smelled the acrid remnants of the explosion, not quite dissipated yet by the steady suck and hiss of the air ducts.

A low scraping sound came from inside the vault. Durell listened for the sound of Jessie Corbin's voice. He didn't hear it. She wasn't here; she wasn't interested in the money. She would be busy elsewhere. He was sure Slago or Fleming was in the vault. They had no hint of his presence. Durell touched Angelina and backed quietly out of the huge circular room. Her eyes shot a question at him, but he shook his head quickly for silence.

In the corridor outside he paused, looked at his watch. Angelina whispered: "But they're in there. *He's* in there. Slago. Why don't you—"

"They're not important. They'll be busy for another ten minutes, loading and packing the money. The girl is somewhere else, and she's the one I've got to stop." He looked at Angelina with uncertainty. "Do you think you could hold everything here?"

146

"Alone?"

"I don't have much time. They've split up, and the girl is more important than those two in there." He didn't like to leave her along again. "Never mind," he said. "Stick close to me."

"No, I'll stay," she said. "They won't get out."

He looked at the Luger in her hand. He looked at the steady lift of her eyes. He couldn't spare any more time thinking about it.

"All right," he decided. "When you hear them come out of the vault, close this door. Fire a couple of shots into it, to hold them inside. If they start for you anyway, do whatever is necessary to keep them here. Do you understand?"

She nodded, pushed back her tangled black hair, and even managed a taut smile. "Go ahead, Sam, don't worry about me. I'm all right."

He moved away from her down the empty corridor. At the first turn, he looked back. She was holding the gun in both hands, pointed at the big door to the circular room. She wasn't looking at him at all. . . .

Later, when he dreamed about the next few minutes' search, it followed the familiar pattern of racing and hunting through a morbid, deserted world, as if he were the last man left alive. Everywhere he saw the silently operating machines, working on automation, a mechanical industry and a calm patience that was unhuman and unnatural. There were long steel stairways spiraling deeper into new abysses, more corridors, barracks, mess rooms, and offices. He ignored everything but the military units. Wherever he saw a restricted sign, he entered, searched, and went on.

Finally he came to where an army major lay slumped over a desk. The door stood open beyond the unconscious man. To the left, an atomic warning sign was blazoned over a long, downward ramp where Durell guessed the power plant was located. He ignored that and pushed past the unconscious major. This was the heart of it all, the reason for the existence of all this elaborate paraphernalia. Durell glanced at the long tables, the computing machines, the maps and charts and pinpointed SAC airbases, Nike sites, and more symbols that he guessed were launching bases for intercontinental ballistic missiles. It was all here, faithfully reproduced, in a sweeping panorama of silent efficiency that was designed to reduce confusion and permit those in charge of national security to carry on with a minimum of delay.

And here was Jessie Corbin, too.

S HE stood with her back to him, under a bank of pale yellow lamps, and she took a flat tray of charts out of a cabinet before her. She was using a miniature camera, snapping shot after shot of the entire defense pattern. Her blonde head was bent forward over her task. She wore dark slacks and a thin sweater and she had a large leather shoulder bag slung against her hip. She gave no sign of being aware of his entrance behind her. She took one more flash picture, rolled the tray of charts back, and set her camera for another, then paused to glance at her watch.

Durell said: "I think you've taken quite enough."

His voice held a harsh, echoing quality in the huge room. Jessie Corbin didn't move at once. She stood still, and Durell lifted his gun and watched her holding the camera in both hands. Then she put it down carefully on the map tray. Turning, she smoothed her palms on the thighs of her slacks.

"So you've found us," she said quietly.

"Did you think I wouldn't?"

"We should have left the girl with you. That was my mistake," she said. "It would have satisfied you long enough to put you far behind us."

"No."

"Have you found her?"

"Yes."

"Then I have nothing to bargain with, have I?"

"There was never any chance to bargain," Durell said. "Move away from the charts, please. Put your camera on the table there."

She did as she was told. He could read very little in her face. Her pale violet eyes looked up at him once, shockingly hard and cold, and that was all.

"Now come with me. We don't have much time."

"Nine minutes."

"Who were you going to sell your films to?" he asked.

"Anybody," she said. "I don't care who the buyers may be. The obvious customers, of course, are the people behind the Iron Curtain. But I've had offers from other sources that would surprise you. From people the State Department regards as friendly. You would be

148

amazed at how many so-called neutrals, and even allies, would like to know what America's defense plans actually are."

"And you'd sell to the highest bidder?"

Her mouth twisted. "Don't moralize to me, Durell. I don't know who you are, but I can guess. I made the mistake of thinking you were just a small-time crook from the bayous, out for an easy dollar. I didn't quite classify you with Slago and Fleming, but close enough to have made my major error. Can we bargain at all?"

"No."

She picked up the camera again, weighing it in her hands. She was surprisingly calm, and this worried Durell, because he had expected violence from her in last-minute defeat. She said: "There's a lot of money represented in these films, but it isn't for the money that I did all this. I wasn't ever treated right, you know. I never had a decent chance. I had to sell myself for anything I ever got, and even then I was cheated and thrown aside afterward. I made up my mind long ago that I would get even for the kind of rotten life I had over here. I guess you know all about what I've been doing in Europe."

"Some of it," Durell admitted. "You've had a lifelong jag of self-pity, haven't you?"

"I never got a break, I tell you!" she said angrily. "With these films, it doesn't matter what happens to me afterward. Maybe you think everything here can be changed around in time. But it's too complicated, and you know it. It would take months, even a year or more, to relocate all the bases and redesign the defense plans. With these films in the hands of my buyers, this country wouldn't get the chance to plan a new setup."

"Your buyers aren't going to get them," Durell said.

"I think they will. You can't stop me."

"I'll take the camera now," Durell said. "Put it down on the table and walk over to the wall."

She didn't move. She seemed to be waiting for something.

WHATEVER she was waiting for didn't happen. Not just then. Durell looked beyond her and saw the charts and diagrams and organizational tables, the huge plot map of the United States and most of the Northern Hemisphere, with buttons indicating bases and long radii reaching out to other parts of the globe, pointing the way toward retaliation. He saw Jessie Corbin's angry face, the intelligent violet eyes, the harsh red mouth.

"Where did you learn about this place?" he asked.

"From a man."

"From a traitor. In Washington?"

"You won't learn his name from me."

"I think we will, Mrs. Corbin. We'll learn a lot from you. You're going to tell us who gave you the information that brought you to this place and why he gave it to you and where we can pick him up. You'll tell us all that and everything else, before the sun goes down."

"You'll be dead by then," she said quietly.

"And in a few minutes the garrison here is going to start waking up."

"That's right."

"How do you expect to get out?"

"I know a way."

"You don't really know anything," Durell said. "All you know is your futile grievance because of your own failures. You tell yourself you've been cheated by a system that never gave you a chance, but if you were honest you'd admit that the failure was in you, and nowhere else. Yet you're willing to smash everything for a moment's revenge. You're ready to see millions die and more millions suffer in agony. I don't understand you. I don't know how you could do what you've tried to do. I don't feel sorry for you. I don't feel any pity. What's going to happen to you is only what you've asked for yourself."

"We'll see," she said.

"We'll find your real accomplices. I know Slago and Fleming aren't important. Neither is Erich, really. But the man who gave you those blueprints is, and you're going to tell us where to look for him."

He had been waiting and listening through the sound of his voice for another sound, of any kind, from Angelina. But he hadn't heard anything. And now he knew that too much time had gone by, and there should have been something, perhaps the crash of Angelina's Luger, because Slago and Fleming knew the time limit and would be starting out by now. But he hadn't heard a thing.

And then, as Jessie smiled, he heard the footstep behind him.

Chapter Twenty

D URELL did not know where it had gone wrong, and there was no time to think or wonder about it.

"Drop it, Durell."

Durell lowered his gun, but he did not let go of it. The voice had been harsh and angry, and he guessed it was Fleming. Not Slago. He did not hear Slago's footsteps. He wondered desperately what had gone wrong with Angelina, and then Jessie said in a flat voice: "Durell is with the FBI or something like that, Mark. Kill him, please."

"You've seen him before," Fleming said. "How do you know so much about him, Jessie?"

"Don't waste time talking," the woman snapped. We've got only a few minutes to get out of here." She picked up the camera. "Hurry, Mark."

Fleming said: "Did you get everything you wanted, baby?"

"Yes. Now get this over with and let's go."

"Slago didn't get what he wanted," Fleming said. "Neither did I."

In the momentary silence, Durell turned a little. He could see Fleming now, in the doorway to the plotting room. He stood directly under one of the fluorescent light tubes that shone down on his yellow curly hair and made strange shadows on his round, boyish face. His mouth was ugly. His gun was pointed at a spot between Durell and Jessie Corbin, and he was looking at the woman with hatred.

"What is it?" Jessie said. She held the camera to her breast. "What's the matter with you, Mark?"

"It's the money," Fleming said. "Millions of it. It was all there, all right, just as you said. Only it's no good."

"No good?"

"It's all been printed on special plates, with new engravings. It's marked 'Emergency Currency.' Right now it isn't worth the paper it's printed on. Look at it!"

He tossed a packet of currency with his left hand. It

151

landed on the table and went sliding and turning along the polished surface toward the woman standing behind it. Jessie Corbin's eyes followed the money as if hypnotized. Mark Fleming looked at it, too.

Durell shot Fleming in the left knee, shot him again in the right arm.

The sound of his gun raised smashing echoes in the underground room. Fleming went down as if his leg had been yanked out from under him, and the gun in his hand went clattering to the tiled floor. He began to scream before the echoes died away, staring wide-eyed at his shattered leg. Durell spun around toward Jessie Corbin at the table. She wasn't there. She was running for a door at the far end of the plotting chamber, carrying her precious camera. Durell raised his gun, then lowered it. He couldn't shoot her. She knew too much. She knew the name of the traitor in Washington.

Fleming's screams followed him as he plunged into a back corridor behind the plotting room. Apparently Jessie Corbin knew exactly where she was going; she had thoroughly memorized the blueprints to this maze. He glimpsed her as she darted through another doorway, and as Durell ran after her through the exit, a man on his hands and knees got in his way and Durell stumbled and fell over him and slammed hard against the wall. The man was an army sergeant, crawling stolidly toward a telephone on a desk in the corridor. The thought touched Durell that Corbin's gas was wearing off a few minutes earlier than expected. In a few more moments, all hell would break loose as the stunned garrison came back to life. There would be no time for questions or arguments with the aroused guards. They would shoot first at any stranger they saw.

He raced on after Jessie Corbin. There was a long stairway ahead, at the end of the corridor, and instead of climbing them to an upper level nearer the surface, she darted downward. Durell sprinted, glimpsed her as she turned a corner in the far depths, and heard a low, moaning alarm siren groan into life. More of the garrison members were coming to. He hit the stairs hard, his left hand sliding on the bannister, spinning on the newel posts at each landing. He had no idea where the girl was heading. Possibly for an elevator she knew about down here. She still had the camera, and he yelled her name, ordering her to halt. She didn't bother to look back. She was more than fifty feet ahead of him, running down a long ramp at the foot of the stairway, when he fired a shot over her head. Her body flinched, but she didn't stop. There was a door ahead, with large red warnings printed above it, and she yanked it open and ducked through. Durell looked at the atomic insigne and plunged after her.

He was in another huge, circular room, standing upon a gallery that ran high around the circumference of the pit below. The walls were tiled in ceramic white. More warning signs were hung everywhere. A technician in a white smock was standing dazedly on the floor of the pit far below the railing where Durell halted and looked down. The man was scratching his head and looking around as if wondering what had hit him. Durell saw the bank of instruments down there, the lights flickering, saw the massive wall of the atomic reactor, the shielded pipes, the dials and the controls, the doors on the gallery opposite the door he had entered.

He did not see Jessie Corbin.

The technician shouted something from the floor below, and his voice reached Durell in garbled, querulous echoes. He didn't bother to reply. He looked to right and left, searching for the woman. Panic touched him, lest he lose her. There were other doors, some painted red, some yellow, all closed. She had vanished behind one of them, ducking off the gallery. He chose the one that read, *Emergency Exit,* spun on his heel, slapped the swinging panel open, and went through.

THEY were waiting for him here. It was a small room, painted yellow, with an archway beyond leading to another gallery that in turn opened onto a conventional power plant that drew the steam for its turbines from the atomic generator behind him. This was the source of the steady pulsing pressure of energy he had felt far up on the surface, before his descent.

"Come on in, buddy boy."

He saw Slago and Angelina. Jessie Corbin was punching the buttons of an emergency elevator set into a recess beside the archway. Her face looked pale and savage. Slago had Angelina's gun. He held her with one massive forearm locked around her waist.

Angelina made a gasping sound. "Don't worry about me, Sam. Please."

153

Jessie looked at Durell and said to Slago: "What are you waiting for? Take him! He got Mark—"

"The elevator won't work," Durell said. "Drop the gun, Slago. The garrison is waking up. Mark can't help you, either. Nobody can help you now. You can't get out of here."

He saw that Slago was not going to surrender. He knew that Slago was the kind who would fight with insane violence to the bitter end. He yelled wildly a split second before a tiny facial spasm warned him that Slago was going to shoot. At the same moment he lunged to one side, driving into Angelina. Slago's gun slammed explosively, but Durell's yell had jolted him, and he missed. Durell kept driving, forcing Angelina between them, feeling her twist and claw at Slago in her effort to escape. Jessie Corbin shrank away to one side. The elevator wasn't coming. One hand touched her throat, and her other hand still held the camera.

Slago tried to club at Durell with the Luger, and hit Angelina instead, and the girl suddenly became a dead weight falling back against Slago. Slago tripped, shouted a curse, and stumbled against the wall. Durell's gun barked once, and he knew the bullet had gone home. Slago turned, staggering toward an iron stairway at the arch that opened into the power plant. The man had the strength of an ox, the persistence of a bull. His face was white and his eyes were hooded as he grabbed at the iron railing. He was going to climb down into the pit below. Durell plunged after him, felt the heavy blow of Slago's forearm slam across the bridge of his nose. Slago's gun fell and clattered to the steel plates of the floor far below. Durell hit him, using a judo cut that would have paralyzed any ordinary man, but Slago was beyond ordinary reactions. His breath came in a quick, gasping puff and then he reached out and snatched Durell to him and they both slipped and staggered down the first few steel treads of the spiral staircase. The man's strength was frenzied. A steady stream of bitter curses came from him. Durell could not break his grip. He felt himself starting to fall—and then he felt a sudden jolt and he was abruptly free of Slago's weight.

Angelina had done it.

She had picked herself up, circled behind him, gotten to the stairs and tripped Slago. The man screamed as he

154

lost his grip on the steep treads. For a few steps he went stumbling downward, his arms flailing at the air, and then he hit the rail and fell over backward. He did not stop screaming until his body struck the steel floor in front of the turbines far below.

Durell leaned over the rail and looked down at him. His breath came in agonized gasps. Slago wasn't moving. The man looked as if his back were broken. Durell looked at Angelina, clinging to the stair rail, sobbing, the anger fading from her eyes. He looked for Jessie Corbin. The blonde woman still stood at the elevator, punching at the button. Durell walked over to her and took the camera away.

The sound of the siren ended. Somewhere a whistle began to blow shrilly and authoritatively. Durell heard the pounding tread of running feet, attracted by his shot, and he turned back to Angelina.

"Thanks. . . . Are you all right?"

"Yes . . . yes."

He looked down at Slago. "You don't have to worry about him any more. How did they get by you?"

"There was another door. Fleming came around behind me and took me by surprise. I wanted—I wanted to die. I thought I'd failed you . . ." She looked below and shuddered. "Slago was going to drag you down there with him."

"But he didn't. I owe you something for that."

He had no time to say more just then. An irate army major, followed by three of the guards, came storming into the room, pistols drawn. Durell dropped his gun to the floor and spoke quietly and rapidly to them, before one of the trigger-happy men could decide to shoot him.

IT WAS three o'clock in the afternoon. Durell had been on the telephone speaking to Wittington and Kincaid, and he had had another hour's talk with the colonel in charge of Kittitimi Mountain. Slago was dead. Mark Fleming was in the hospital at Groversville, under police guard. Erich Corbin was in the local sheriff's jail, along with Jessie. While Durell had answered the colonel's questions, exercising care in telling just so much and no more, MacCreedy had come in with two more FBI men. MacCreedy looked as young and jaunty as before, but his eyes were hard and uncompromising when he

155

asked Durell to get into his car and drive down the mountain into the town.

"There's going to be hell raised in Washington over this," MacCreedy said. "The FBI has all jurisdiction over domestic counterespionage, as you damned well know. You didn't tell me a thing back in New Orleans, but you might be interested to know that we had you under surveillance for most of your route."

"Then why didn't you show up when I needed you?" Durell asked.

MacCreedy gave him a cigarette. "There was a minor sort of snafu. It doesn't matter now. Anyway, you've got a lot of explaining to do."

"Not me. Ask Wittington about it. Or your chief."

"Now, look, I can't go to him and complain—"

"I'm tired," Durell said. "I'm happy to leave all the rest of it to you. You've got Mrs. Corbin's camera, haven't you? You've got her in jail? Have you talked to her yet?"

"I'm going there now."

"She's got a lot to tell you," Durell said, "but most of it you won't be able to use in the trial or in newspaper headlines. But the rest of it is up to you. Somebody gave her the blueprints to Kittitimi, and you'll have to make her talk about it."

"She'll talk," MacCreedy said. "Leave that to us."

Durell said, "What did your man do with Angelina?"

"She's at Amberley's house, for now. He'll be all right, by the way. In bed for a month, but he'll be fine. His doctor looked after your girl."

"Drop me off there," Durell said.

THE Canadian geese were still feeding the reeds along the shores of the lake. Amberley's house looked the same, except that now the Jaguar stood in the sweeping driveway in front of the yellow door, instead of being parked in the carport. Durell saw Mrs. Amberley moving behind the big window wall facing the lake. She opened the front door before he got to it.

"Your girl is down there," Mrs. Amberley said.

Durell looked to where she pointed and saw a faint movement down by the shore of the lake. He thanked her and walked that way and saw Angelina seated on the grassy bank of the lake, her back resting against a tall pine. He sat down beside her.

156

"Hello."

She looked at him and said his name and looked at the water. She had changed her clothes. The dress did not fit her too well, since it was a little too small, and when she saw him looking at it, she said: "The FBI left me here to rest and get checked over by Mr. Amberley's doctor. This dress belongs to Mrs. Amberley's daughter. I must look awful."

"You look fine," Durell said.

"Are you all right, Sam?"

"I'm tired," he said. "But it's all over, and that makes me feel better. The FBI is going to take it all from here."

"Slago is dead, I hear. Did I kill him, Sam?"

"You helped."

She shivered suddenly. "I thought it wouldn't bother me, because I thought it would make me happy just to know he was dead. But I'm sorry I had to do it. I didn't want to, but I had to, didn't I? He would have killed you."

"He was trying pretty hard," Durell admitted.

She looked down and hugged her knees and then plucked at a handful of grass and let it trickle through her fingers. "What will you do now, Sam?"

"I have to go back to Washington; they're waiting for my report. I don't know what the next job will be."

"I've been thinking, Sam. The past is all over, isn't it? I ought to forget it, too."

"Not all of it," he said.

"Yes, all of it," she insisted. "Yesterday and today and years ago, too. That's the only way to do it. I thought for a while that I didn't want to live any more. I was in love with you, as I used to be in the old days, and after Slago did— Afterward, I thought you'd never want me again, and there was no use in living any more. But if I could forget it, maybe I could start all over again. Do you think I could, Sam?"

"I'm sure of it."

She turned suddenly to look at him. "Would you kiss me, Sam?"

He kissed her. She clung to him fiercely, and when she let go she was crying. "You didn't mind, Sam?"

"You said you were going to forget."

"It's not easy. I may need help."

Durell thought of the men in Washington who were waiting impatiently for him to make his report. He ought to be with MacCreedy, interrogating Jessie Corbin, trying to wind up the loose ends, keeping himself busy.

But he didn't want to go anywhere. He looked at the Canadian geese and threw a pebble into the lake and watched the ripples move out in widening circles touched by the warm afternoon sunlight. Everything you said and did made circles like that, like a pebble dropped into a pool, and there was never any end to it. The little waves kept going out and out, away from the middle where the pebble or the word had been dropped, or where the deed had been done, but after a time there really was no trace in the water where the pebble, the word, or the deed had been.

"I'll help you, Angelina," he said.

"But you have to go back to Washington."

"Let them wait," he said.

THE END
of an Original Gold Medal Novel by
EDWARD S. AARONS

Even on the witness stand, the one thing she dared not deny was her overwhelming sensuality

NOT I, SAID THE VIXEN

by Bill S. Ballinger

W *was the mystery beauty in the Red Jay?*
prowled the world of twilight women?
H *ruined her lovers with the hot breath of scandal?*
was the frightened seductress in 3-A?
O *committed the city's most sensational murder?*

NOT I, SAID THE VIXEN
But the State was determined to prove otherwise.

Not since WITNESS FOR THE PROSECUTION has there been such a shattering novel of courtroom drama.

k1529 40¢

on sale wherever paperbacks are available

BIGGER THAN ALL OUTDOORS . . .

WILDER THAN HELL ON WHEELS . . .

Harry Julian Fink's

MAJOR DUNDEE

A brilliant, towering story of one extraordinary man whose bitter, savage mission was to hunt down a band of kill-crazy Apaches—to track them through the burning deserts, through the snowbound mountain passes, into the God-forgotten wastes of a country that ate men raw.

But the land and the Indians were not all Dundee had to survive. There were the men in his own command; brawling Union troops, smoldering Rebel prisoners, blood-hungry civilian renegades, a convicted murderer—and a Confederate officer who was Dundee's sworn enemy.

A NOVEL YOU CANNOT AFFORD TO MISS . . .

A MOTION PICTURE YOU'LL NEVER FORGET

Harry Julian Fink's

MAJOR DUNDEE

k1519   **40¢**

on sale wherever paperbacks are
available